PENGUIN BOOKS

A Parish of Rich Women

James Buchan is the son and grandson of writers. He read Persian and Arabic at Magdalen College, Oxford, and from 1978 to 1982 reported from the Middle East for the *Financial Times*. He edited the manuscript of *The House of Saud* left by David Holden at his assassination, and helped Richard Johns to complete this memorial to Holden. He is now *Financial Times* correspondent in Bonn. James Buchan's book on the Greens in West Germany will be published this year. *A Parish of Rich Women* won the David Higham Prize for Fiction, 1984, and the Whitbread Literary Award for the Best First Novel 1984–5.

JAMES BUCHAN

A PARISH
OF RICH WOMEN

Penguin Books

Penguin Books Ltd, Harmondsworth, Middlesex, England
Viking Penguin Inc., 40 West 23rd Street, New York, New York 10010, U.S.A.
Penguin Books Australia Ltd, Ringwood, Victoria, Australia
Penguin Books Canada Ltd, 2801 John Street, Markham, Ontario, Canada L3R 1B4
Penguin Books (N.Z.) Ltd, 182–190 Wairau Road, Auckland 10, New Zealand

First published by Hamish Hamilton Ltd 1984
Published in Penguin Books 1985

Made and printed in Great Britain by
Cox & Wyman Ltd, Reading
Typeset in Bembo

For the fallen of this parish

A PARISH
OF RICH WOMEN

CHAPTER ONE

It was the summer before that first big summer of weddings because Adam was in London; and not simply in London this first early summer evening but hesitating before the closed front door of a house in Hans Place and quite drunk.

Adam was often drunk at this time. He had been abroad a year but nobody much wanted to hear about it, least of all Mary, who did not like abroad and could manage only a smile of puzzled sympathy. Even Johnny, who knew the city well, always broke him off.

Adam found it simpler to be drunk some of the time. No one minded and Mary, in a queer way, even encouraged him; but Adam did not yet have much idea why she did one thing rather than another. She was too young to have habits and they had been known to each other for just two weeks.

It was that hot summer of 198–, the summer of the war, because David was giving a party and feeble tapers flickered each side of the closed front door. Adam did not like David Lowestoft, or did not see what he was for, unless it was to give large parties in his house in Hans Place to which many were asked and more came and where Adam might find his friends.

Johnny's dog was running at Catford and Toby had convinced himself, and eventually Mary, that they could not lose; but Adam, worried by guilt over a book he was trying to write, had stayed behind at Clements Street. Yet the press cuttings he had laid out in a space on the dining-room table, the notes of old conversations in shelters or requisitioned houses, had lost all actuality as if separated by a long journey during part of which he had slept. He had drunk Mary's whisky; he had forced himself back, turning onto the Corniche, with the sea on his left hand and the

3

shuttered Lunapark black against the horizon; but his steps had taken him miles, to a ruined apartment block, to a piece of open ground. Adam had got up and walked to David's.

He looked round at the trees waving in the square garden and back at the sacramental tapers. He turned again but the door sprang open and a gust of alcohol obliterated the square.

'What was the name, please?' A desk blocked Adam's way and behind it a large man with a beard and black coat. Behind him, men and women moved to and fro.

'Adam Murray.'

The butler worked slowly down M on a typed list. 'You're not on the list. You aren't asked,' he said, standing up.

'Mr Lowestoft telephoned me this afternoon.'

The butler looked at Adam. Adam looked at the floor. His suit, he now saw with the butler's eye, was not right although white and linen and cut by old M. Habib himself as a break from an order for uniforms patterned with parachutes and tanks. Crumpled and harmlessly colonial, Adam had thought of the suit at the time. His hair, a good civilian length over there, was too long for this year in London. His face, after a year abroad, was unfashionably pale.

'What was the name again, Sir?' The butler added Adam in ink to the bottom of the list, just below Toby, and smiled. 'Mr Lowestoft can afford one more. Anyway, some tart's passed out already.'

Adam walked past him into the party.

What a room it was and what a crowd! There were so many people, young, middle-aged, even decrepit; standing in pairs or small groups or alone with their backs to the red, dragged walls or staring out of the two big windows or kneeling on the hearth rug or sitting on the club fender; talking or saying nothing or laughing, some loudly with a bending back at the waist, some softly with a leaning forward into their drinks; and the clothes they were wearing, no uniforms but the men in black or white dinner-jackets or red or blue smoking-jackets or striped suits or blazoned tee-shirts, and the women in coloured artificial

4

trousers or shorts and fishnet stockings or white or black dresses to the carpet, some with bare shoulders and some with bare bellies and some covered up to the neck; and, here, two young men in the middle with space about them, all in black leather with pieces of metal hanging down and short haircuts and tiny moustaches, rolling their bottoms in time to each other; and there, three little girls with spiky hair and torn plastic dresses, drinking from broken glasses and snarling. The smoking was furious.

The other large room was older and less drunk, as if human beings find a level like oil in a glass. Great old ladies had been seated on high-backed chairs and encircled by men, who sat on the floor and hugged their knees and laughed like boys hearing about brave Sir Walter.

Adam's friends were not there. They were not in the kitchen where boys sat on dressers and gave hostile hellos, or on the stairs, where girls sat clutching packets of cigarettes and queued to pee, or in the bathroom on the landing where David Lowestoft was lifting bottles of champagne from a bath of ice.

'Hello, David.'

'Hello, Adam.' David looked pleased with the world. 'Have a bottle, though it's not very nice, is it?' He drew the cork out quietly. 'Heidsieck makes you sick. But one never listens.'

To Adam, David's voice always sounded curiously flat as if he were hiding a defect of speech. 'Have you seen Mary?'

'Somewhere. Sweet girl, isn't she, and such a good eye. I'm delighted with the Watteau drawing, though it cost a fair amount, I can tell you.'

'Dream tart.'

'Dream tart?' David swilled the phrase round his large mouth exactly as he must have been doing for some time with his sweet champagne, trying to draw encouragement. Tortoiseshell spectacles flashed in his fat face. 'You know she brought some people with her.'

'That would be Toby and Johnny. They went dog-racing at Catford.'

'No. I told Henry not to let them in. It's perfectly fair. I warned them last time.'

5

'That's a bit hard, isn't it?'

'No. I've had enough. I have to think of the others. Princess Margaret was going to come. I don't mind Laura coming. She's a,' he giggled and swilled some wine round his mouth, 'a dream tart too. She's not responsible for her brother, though why she runs around with Toby, I can't understand.'

'They're my friends,' said Adam. 'Who did Mary bring?'

'Short and losing his hair. Rather a rat. And some girl.'

'Oddjob.'

'Oddjob?' David swilled the unusual name.

'Oliver Thwaite. I wonder why. Sells insurance. Laura loathes him.'

'You know the girl has passed out in the loo.' His voice fell to a whisper and he took a step closer. 'Do you think we should break the door down? She might, you know, suffocate on her own vomit.' David giggled at the violence of his language.

'If she is being sick . . .'

'She might be being sick.' David struggled between conscience and torpor. 'Oh, it's early yet. Shall we leave her for a bit? Come and shoot in August. Or aren't you going back to the Middle East, I heard.'

'No. I'm not. And I don't know how to shoot.'

'Morocco, is it? I'll talk to Mary about Scotland.'

David returned to his sad tasting and Adam to his search. In the bedroom next door, three girls were playing three-handed bridge on a hillock of coats. As Adam entered, Laura got up with that strange movement of hers, half-lion cub and half-serpent, and peered at him closely. 'Oh, it's you Adam. Come in. Adam can play my hand. I want to pee.'

'I'm looking for Mary, actually.'

The other girls glared at him. 'Haven't seen the festering tart. You dealt, Laura. You must open. Go away, Adam.'

Laura turned back reluctantly. 'I must talk to you. Something has happened.'

'Some girl's passed out. I know that.'

'No. No. About Johnny,' she said and peered down to arrange her cards.

It was not that Laura was not interested in the outside world, Adam thought as he climbed the last flight of stairs. She was, passionately. In the five years he had known her and Johnny, he had often seen her with spectacles of clumsy design; but there would be transparent tape where earpiece met lens; and the next time, there would be no earpiece on one side; and the next, she would rise with her serpentine movement and look him closely in the face. Whereas Johnny never left a mark behind him, and sometimes sat so still one thought he had left the room, Laura could be tracked round Clements Street by the disorder of her short sight; a book out of the shelves, a discarded shoe, a turd of ash on a cigarette she could not find.

In the bedroom at the top of the stairs, Adam saw a down-at-heel pair of shoes before he saw Toby himself, lying fully clothed between the sheets with a small smile on his face. He was asleep. Adam quietly crossed the room and looked out at the streetlamps in the square. What a good part of London it was! Behind the curtained windows, Adam conjured shawled women on watered-silk sofas and children picking at nursery wallpaper. A cry from downstairs disturbed him. He drew the curtains on the streetlamps and closed the door softly behind him.

The stairs were empty. The players had put their cards down in three untidy piles on the hill of coats. David had abandoned his bottles, the young girls gone from their stations. For all Adam knew, whoever it was had risen heavily from the floor of the loo and even Toby somehow emerged, fully clothed, from bed as refreshed by his short sleep as the hero of a thriller. The rude young men had evacuated the kitchen.

Everybody was in the big room where the dowagers had sat. There was nothing to see but shoulders and heads but, going up on his toes, Adam felt a ripple of movement. It was like wind in tall grass or the reluctant break in a crowd when the ambulance arrived at last, the escorts firing crazily in the air. Adam turned away and saw Mary, standing with Laura at the buffet, eating something. 'What happened, Mary?'

'Oddjob has killed that poor Poppy-tart. The butler had to break the window from outside.'

'My God, dead?'

'Well all but. I suppose he gave her a few mandrax hoping to have his heart's desire but it was not to be.' Mary Mark sighed. 'Biology supervened. Just like with poor Laura, last time.' Mary did not need to speak over the noise from the room. The tone of her voice was penetrating. Adam did not find it unpleasant, simply unusual.

'Why did you bring him, Mary? Why? Why?' Laura peered at them in turn.

'Oh Laura, don't fuss. It's just that that David is so pompous.' Laura turned away and stared vaguely into the garden. She seemed upset.

Adam turned back to Mary. 'Where were you? I looked all over for you.'

'Why?' She put down her smoked turkey and wiped her fingers neatly on Adam's trousers.

Adam started to think but soon gave up. 'Because you're my tart, that's why.'

Mary Mark smiled and with her two little fingers hitched her pink dress to her chin. Adam looked away. Everybody about looked away and, as they all turned, caught a flash of grey stocking on white leg and remembered it as they went on talking absently.

'Mary, don't do that. Nobody's interested.' Mary dropped her dress. They had drifted away from Laura to the pudding sector of the buffet. Adam felt alarm for M. Habib's trousers.

'Do you know what Oddjob has really got?' Mary spoke as softly as her voice would allow.

'Yes.' He had not but did now.

'Shouldn't we get some? For Helle, I mean, at the weekend. The thing is I gave all my cash to To at Catford.'

'I doubt it.'

'You may be right.' She moved a step closer, though whether in affection or obedience, Adam could not tell.

Oliver pushed through to join them. He was so short that his appearance in crowds was unexpected. Unheralded by head or wave, he appeared at chest level, as if he had sprung

8

from the earth but caught on something. Despite his modest job, Oliver always dressed beautifully, but this evening he did not look well. His face, and even the exposed parts of his scalp, were white and his left eye twitched. 'Rather tired,' he said heavily.

'Why did you kill her,' Laura said, turning back to them. 'You mustn't try and kill her. She probably has a mother.'

'Just a bit tired, that's all. Go home. Princess Margaret.'

'Oliver wouldn't kill anybody, would you, dear?' Mary put her arm round his shoulder. Oliver, who hardly reached Mary's bosom even when they were seated, smiled to himself and brushed down the sparse strands of hair that crossed his bald spot. How they had become disarranged, Adam could not imagine, unless Mary had been patting his head all evening as if she were an infanta and he some half-witted palace dwarf. She picked up a profiterole and began to feed him. Adam turned away.

The room was now emptying. The dowagers had vanished and Adam recognised nobody beyond the safety of the buffet. He did not like open spaces and he made for the cover of the door with an air of deep resolution. In the hall, he glanced for the last time up the stairs and saw Toby, translated from the bedroom, alert and no more crumpled than usual, looking down with pleasure at the milling heads below him.

'Did you have a good sleep?'

'Outstanding. I needed to lie down for a moment and the fellow at the door said I should keep out of sight for a bit. Quite reasonable here, isn't?' Toby sighed with pleasure.

'Actually, I'm off. I don't suppose you've got the Clements Street key, have you?'

'What do you mean? You can't just leave.' Toby squared his shoulders and pushed his hips forward. 'We've only begun phase two of the evening. You can't just bale out.'

'Did Chatila's Darling win?'

'Are you mad? Went backwards. Johnny accused the starters of putting a burr up its bum. Still, he managed to sell it to some bloke. 150 quid. Not bad.'

'What on earth for? I thought Johnny loved that dog.'

'He needs the money. He's going off tomorrow.'

9

'Well he might have come and said goodbye.'

'Oh, you know Johnny. The point about him is that he's a low-lifer, not like us. He hates this sort of thing,' Toby made a large gesture over the heads: 'This human caviar, a reviving dose of class hatred. He said he'd see you there.'

'Where? Where's he going? When?'

'I don't know. He was a bit plastered. Laura and Mary kicked up a fuss because we went to a pub.'

'Come on, Toby. Where?'

'Is there a museum there? At the museum, I think. He said that a couple of times. Bloody stupid.'

Adam sat down on the stairs. 'Bloody stupid,' he said.

'Ha. Feeling a bit upstaged, are we? I wouldn't worry. He dropped a few dark hints; you know what he's like when he's had a drop; he's probably only washing up in that hotel. What's it called?'

'The Admiral,' Adam said. 'I haven't got any plans to go back. I have to finish the book. It's impossible there. The security situation is terrible. Unless you stay on the eastern side and they're such shits.' Adam stopped talking to himself and looked up. 'Does Laura know?'

'Well, she came the sister thing a bit. She'll be all right. I think it could be rather nice. Can one drink there?'

'To death.'

'Talking of which, I hear old Oddjob has been up to his tricks. Mary insisted we bring him.'

Adam could not reply for Mary was advancing up the stairs towards them, leading Oliver by the hand. His cheeks were smeared with chocolate. Behind them came Laura, still abstracted.

'Oliver dear, Adam is interested in what you've got,' Mary said. Her progress up the stairs had obliged Adam and Toby to retreat to the landing. In the silence that followed her remark, Adam felt walls meet at his back.

'Great conversationalists, aren't we?' said Toby.

'It's 60 quid,' said Oliver fluently.

'Well, I've got nine from Catford.' Toby drew out from his coat a small wad of old pound notes.

'No,' said Adam.

'Come on, darling. You've got all that money from the Guineas. Don't be so mean.'

Adam looked down at Laura. Her blue eyes were quite blank. Nothing and nobody stays still, he thought and walked up the stairs.

They sat in the room where Toby had slept. There was a key in the brass lock, and while Adam gave all the money he could find to Oliver, Toby set to work, cutting up the stuff on an ormolu mirror he had taken from the wall. Laura lay with her face in the pillows. Mary strode up and down, looking without concentration at the large nudes on the walls.

'Dirty bloke, that David. All labia,' she said and then peered over Toby's shoulder. 'I shan't have much.'

'Yes, you will.' Toby chuckled.

Adam walked to the window and parted the curtain. A little light was coming into the sky above the solid, red houses. Such a good, safe part of London; and how he had thought of it, every evening, of England and order.

'Don't do that with your teeth.' Mary had put her arms round his neck, not hard, but hard enough to bring his head against her cheek. She turned him round. 'Poor Adam is still a bit war-torn.'

Toby turned and held out the mirror, brandishing his razor-blade like a cutlass. Adam saw five pinkish-grey lines snaking across the old glass and his own face beyond. Beyond that, he saw uniforms and children with tangled hair and dirty faces and trees busted by shellfire and, beyond that, a man stopped still in the middle of an open space as if he had remembered something. Adam closed his eyes.

CHAPTER TWO

The journey to Helle was hard. Adam tried to stay awake but his eyelids were heavy and he kept dipping into a shallow dream that seemed, at his waking with a start, to have been simply the car hurrying west and the fields and small towns it passed. The day was still warm. Adam smelt pasture and petrol. On the far edge of the Chilterns, he saw the distance before them. Oxford was streaks of atrocious colour; white horse-chestnuts, yellow laburnum, mauve lilac. Above the Windrush, he heard the cool splash of water over stones. 'Let's have some beer in Burford, why not?'

'Are you mad?' Mary drove through without a glance down the steep street. 'Dad will kill us if we're late for dinner.' Then she smiled at him. 'Poor Adam. You can get drunk at home. Toby always did.'

'Doesn't your father object?'

'Not really. Billy is too busy with administration for things like guests drinking. My mother does that. She also does administration, come to think of it. Dad does horti-culture.' She smiled at him again and turned back to the road.

The smile covered all of Mary's round, old-fashioned face but the grey eyes did more work than the mouth. When Mary Mark smiled, her upper lip curled diffidently in the middle and showed half a mouth – a glimpse only – of slightly uneven teeth. Adam had never asked about the teeth. The Marks may simply not have noticed that the plump child jamming her face on the nursery lino or playing prettily on the top lawn needed plastic and wire to straight-en her teeth; or perhaps they had something to do with Mary's small limp, an accident out riding or a fall down stairs. The teeth were generally concealed and the closed mouth made for a curious first impression. She was pretty, even Toby admitted; but across a dining-room table, her shoulders bare and moving above a pink silk dress, or striding across David's dance-floor with the smallest suggestion of a roll, she might be someone other than the only daughter of a rich man with a famous house, a waterfront tart, perhaps, with a ponce at home who bashed her up every now and then. This was the first thought that struck Adam the first night he saw her and until a more proud or girlish side appeared – her back was straight and the hand not employed in driving rested neatly in her lap – he had been a little surprised. He had already decided to try and have an affair with her, simply on Toby's report.

Not that Adam would have called himself cold-blooded. Adam never let himself think, or articulate a thought in words his father was fond of using, after lunch, in the smoking-room of the Club, between tales of other men's good wars, that money has a way of sticking to women like Mary as moths are drawn to sugar and molasses. Such raffish Edwardian advice, genuine if a little weary at its third transmission across a generation, appealed to one side of Adam's nature, even though George Murray had taken an immediate dislike to Mary. The other side, his foreign side, approved less and if, in replying to Toby, he sometimes spoke of the difficulty of finding somewhere to live, this was as much distaste at talking about Mary's charm as fear of Toby's scorn. Toby never disguised his dependence on Mary for shelter, and shelter in Chelsea, and Mary liked this.

They would have met anyway but they had met at Harry's, on silk-covered benches set at angles to the bar. Toby had been abusive, for he had seen the turn of events more clearly than they; Laura was miraculously asleep with her head on the bench and her legs drawn up under her; and so they had jumped up and danced by the piano till Mary's legs gave way at the knee and Adam had kissed her, touching with his tongue the strange, uneven teeth. They had danced on, bursting at intervals into small, individual laughs like people who have survived a great danger until Toby fell off his bench and Laura woke with a start . . .

13

'Wake up, Adam.' She was pulling at his arm. 'It's all right for you. You don't have to drive.'

'I'm sorry, Mary. Avenues of naked elms ran out from the roadside or a single blackened tree, encumbered with ivy, stood at a cross-roads as if winter had inherited Wiltshire in perpetuity. They passed long, dilapidated brick walls and park gates boarded with lumber and barbed wire. Adam dabbed his eyelids with spit.

'I don't think we should take that stuff.'

'Toby was sick. On the stairs. David was quite cross.'

'Was that Toby? I couldn't really see by then.'

'Awful, wan't it? Black holes like at the cinema when the film gets burned. Laura thought she was going to die. What did Oddjob put in that thing?'

'Strychnine, I suppose. It's cheaper to mix it in.' Adam remembered his face reflected in the mirror, crossed by the long pink lines and the razor scratches on the old glass, and how, as the blood had taken and run with the drug, he had felt a little tightness in his chest resolve itself, a knot he had not before been aware of, vanish, as if by a tug on the right string. 'That's how he makes his profit.'

'Wicked, wicked Oddjob,' she said.

Adam had not woken that day or had not slept that night but had been in this state of dreaming since Toby had turned round, brandishing his razor-blade like a cutlass. When he opened his eyes at Clements Street, to the dirty window splintered with sunlight, it was with surprise that whole pieces of the night had fallen away and yet he was where he should be. This was a moment which Adam feared, the few seconds before his hangover came out like a bare fist and smashed his hopes for the day. He felt only the dim sensation of something missing, as if he had talked all night. Mary was standing naked before the long wall mirror, admiring herself, her long neck and narrow shoulders converging in a tiny waist, long legs ending in size three feet, each item perfect in itself but the whole a little disjointed, like a yearling standing in a field; from downstairs came the sound and smell of Toby's monstrous breakfast; and Laura was padding in on stockinged feet, avoiding the furniture with exaggerated care . . .

14

'Wake up, you beast.' Mary had leaned right over and was crying with frustration.

'I'm sorry, Mary. I don't think that stuff is terribly good for one.'

Mary smiled pluckily and turned back to the road. Adam looked out into the gloaming. The untidy towns, petrol stations, shaggy allotments had given way to villages, each cottage garden wall tumbling with aubrietia, smooth hills and stands of beech. They hurried over stone bridges decorated with obelisks but spanning tiny streams running down curved beds. It was if some hand, more far-reaching than God or Somerset farmer, had tinkered with the landscape. 'Is this all yours?'

'Could be. Ask mum.'

'Why aren't you lords if you've got all this?'

'Common.'

'But it's odd. You could have bought a title off Lloyd-George or something.'

'Adam, don't bang on. We were once. Always being attainted.'

'What for?'

'Buggery. Treason. The usual things. Ask my mother.'

They rattled over a cattle-grid beside a lodge almost invisible for honeysuckle, slowed down at a corner and, as they rounded it, floodlights came on and showed a house in cream and black, a flash of windows and a gilded cupola, deep beech woods behind. It was as if the car had tripped a wire on the drive or sent some old man in the honeysuckle-encumbered lodge scurrying from tea to telephone.

'Seems all right,' said Adam.

'Now, you must make a good impression. So much depends on it. No more horrid wars; credit at Charvet.'

'I've only got one clean shirt. And bloody Oddjob took all my money.'

'There's no entry fee, you know.' She stopped the car in a scratching of gravel, dived out and ran up a side of the double staircase while Adam shook hands with a butler whom he would have liked one day to have tipped.

*

If Adam was asked what he first remembered from childhood, and it was a common enough question from Laura and Mary who had first met each other at Lady Eden's, he would reply the television pictures of the American fleet off Beirut as he sat watching the early evening news with his mother in the nursery at Brightwell. His friends found this dull or, worse, a crude forgery to justify his later interest in the Palestinians of Lebanon. Yet Adam did remember the occasion clearly, could remember his mother beside him, picking her ears absently with a knitting needle, could hear again strange, round place-names that had broken out from a church smelling of damp: Jerusalem, Sidon, Damascus. There were earlier memories of a domestic nature but Adam could not be sure if he did remember these incidents himself or whether they had been taught him by his mother or sisters or narrated to amuse a guest in the drawing-room at Brightwell. Did he truly remember being struck on the head by his eldest sister or overturning in a double pram with Lydia or falling down dry, sun-bleached steps of a clapboard house they took each year at Bembridge?

What he did remember from about this time, he did not like to tell because it was the end of something he had not known or the beginning of something not yet complete.

It was the early summer of 196–, and late afternoon, for the sunshine was dancing in the drawing room, broken up by the laurel bush outside the window. As he walked in, Adam saw that his mother was not alone. She sat on the sofa, her head thrown back, her eyes closed against the sun. His father sat upright beside her, his arm resting gently on her shoulder. Adam started stepping across the carpet towards her but he must have crossed into a patch of shade made by a laurel branch for his father spoke.

'Adam, old fellow,' he said; and without lifting his arm from his wife's neck, he explained that he was going away on a journey.

To Adam, dressed up, in the drawing room, his head still tingling from the hair-brush, this seemed a sensible plan. He took a quick look at his mother but she could not see him. She merely reached out for his hand and, when he moved forward, patted it.

If Adam, picked up by his sisters and deposited in bed, took the news well, as leaving him, indisputably, the only male in a house full of women, he was not prepared for the next great memory. Adam was now at school in Kent. At half-term or during the holidays, he would have to seek her out in the greenhouse that leaned against the south-facing wall of the house. She would read to him sometimes or knit but usually she sat, her eyes half-closed, soaking up the warmth while petals dropped off one by one from the brilliant geranium she had trained up the wall. Adam would stare at the red cascade, or collect the greasy petals gathering on the flags or look up at the red spots under her sleepy eyes until a word came to him, from out of the knitting bag or *Ivanhoe* or the tubs of geraniums.

'Cancer,' he said but she just reached out for his hand and, when he moved forward, patted it.

The drawing room filled up with men, although these were uncles who took whisky with their tea and his father sat some way apart and did not speak. In the days that followed, other men tramped about the house in wellington boots. They looked at the pictures from all sides and made small jokes to one another. The result of their tramping, and of the tea they, too, had drunk in great quantities, lay in a brown envelope which Adam discovered one day in the drawing-room bureau where his eldest sister had established her clerical activity as mistress of the house. It was not the title – 'Inventory of the contents of Brightwell House, Brightwell' – or the lines at the foot of the page – 'The property of the Misses Lavinia and Lydia Murray and of Master Adam Murray' – which drew Adam to the envelope's drawer in the bureau whenever he was alone in the house. It was to find, in its neat rows of definition and value, the composition of the house at the moments when his father had called him old fellow and when his mother had patted his hand beside the geraniums. In this room was the Bokhara part-saddle-bag, the School of Constable, the Louis XV wall sconces, the square of Wilton carpet, all as he had arranged them and she preserved them. He followed always the route of the inventory, starting with the hall, then passage, kitchen, nursery and drawing room, the bedrooms, and ending before the great picture covering almost half one wall of the dining room, the large naked woman he had grown up to call the Sir Joshua.

'Cupid and Psyche: oil on canvas, Sir Joshua Reynolds . . . £10,000.' Behind the assertion of the inventory, Adam remembered, there had been more than the usual tea, talk and little jokes from the men in gumboots. The picture had at first frightened him as much as the crucifix under its little shelter by the village school, but as the years passed, and he exchanged the church school for prep school and beyond, he was drawn ever more to the elongated figure of Psyche, eyes half-closed and mouth half-open, one hand resting neatly in her groin, and the laughing Cupid peering through the laurel. His sisters, too, bossed by ever more domineering and temporary housekeepers, also fell under the spell of the inventory and would dust with especial care the Sir Joshua, the Louis XV wall sconces and, even, the Pontypool painted coal scuttle. Being older, they also recognised more quickly than Adam that the house was unmanageable and that the half-yearly conferences on their affairs, which took Adam by train from school to offices overlooking the fields at Gray's Inn, were ever more sombre in tone. Adam could not understand how oil prices or the prospects for an American economic recovery affected the house, the laurel bush, the tulip tree almost as big as that at Cliveden or the Sir Joshua, but his uncles were impatient and it was not long before Lavinia was welcoming back the wellingtons.

By the time the sale came round, Adam was resigned and attempted a fifteen-year-old dignity as he showed the county ladies round and heard their harsh comments in execrable schoolgirl French. Inflation had played havoc with the gumboot estimates and many things did well and the 'Attributed to Sir Joshua' particularly so, after a noisy struggle between two Persian dealers to secure her.

Psyche paid for his schooling and his journeys between the uncles in the holidays, and she sent him travelling. A meeting with a Palestinian student in Perugia gave him the notion to go further; by slow stages, he came to Turkey; and, one evening, tumbling sleepily from the cab of a heavy truck, he found himself in a sea of light and a circle of eager faces. The light came from hissing gas-mantle lamps set on barrows of fruit; the faces were the driver's large family who, though Lebanese of Sidon, lived in what had been the Sabra Palestinian refugee camp but was now just a suburb of south Beirut.

For three months, Adam hardly stirred from Sabra for the driver's hospitality was all-embracing and his son, Said, feared to lose Adam to the fleshpots of Ras Beirut or among the Christians of the eastern side. But once, as they walked through the basement of the Museum, Adam saw, from the back, a young European with red hair and had the sensation that they would become friends. Said may well have felt the same for he tried to hurry him on – old things bored Said – but Adam stopped and crouched down beside the boy as a guide with a running nose explained the reliefs on a sarcophagus by the light of a flaring match. Johnny's Arabic was already advanced and, in emulation, Adam devoted a week to learning the Arabic script so that Said's father expressed the hope he might one day read the Koran. Adam did and gained his degree although he fell in with Toby his first day at Oxford, in Johnny's room. Adam could not match Toby's Irish exuberance or Johnny's grasp of the medieval texts served up at Pusey Lane like unappetizing dishes. Whereas Toby never attended a tutorial, and nobody had a clear idea what he was reading, Johnny seemed driven by a demon and would stay at the Oriental Institute till it closed and only then come on to drink with them till he passed out, quite neatly, on the floor of Toby's flat. Fearing to snore or dribble, Adam never attempted this himself.

They travelled together. In Naples, Toby bought dud cocaine while Johnny stole antiquities from unimportant sites. At times, jittery or hungover, Adam thought to hear his friends' voices even in the street. Yet Toby devoted more and more time to Laura while Johnny's bright red hair, viewed through the glass partition of the institute library, warned against interruption.

In the end, Toby was squeezed into a bank in Paris and Johnny started reading for the Foreign Office. All Psyche's money was spent. Both sisters had married quickly, a gentleman historian and a country doctor, dissimilar men but alike in their reasonable incomes. Adam returned to Beirut.

Adam might well have expected to come across the picture again, hanging in a provincial gallery or pointed out by Mary in a sale-room catalogue. He could not have expected to see it at Helle, in the lower passage, as Andrew the butler preceded him with Toby's suitcase. Yet Adam did see, occupying a great space of the passage wall, an elongated female figure, head thrown back, eyes half-closed and mouth half-open, and the boy staring at her through the laurel. He wanted to cry out at his discovery and turned to Andrew, waiting at the corner without impatience, but he did not know what to say or whether Andrew was the person to whom he should say it.

'You will be going straight into dinner.' The remark, phrased between suggestion and question, opened exorbitant possibilities. Might not Adam say no and barricade himself in his room while rich food went cold and old claret sour on the landing outside? But he followed the butler obediently, up a broad flight of steps below the heavenly dome and down a gallery lined with portraits. He was left, hesitating but exultant, by the door of a room full of sound and laughter. Shyness fingered at his stomach.

The room, when he opened the door, was full enough of people; but they turned in their chairs and greeted him with smiles. The men stood up. Only Mary, treacherously changed into a long dress, took no notice as she plied a smiling lady doing needlework with conversation. A woman with silver hair and a light step detached herself and came towards Adam while, from a group of men at the other end of the room, a short, bald fellow in a blue smoking-jacket and slippers bore down on him almost at a run. They came together in a tangle of questions and solicitations, about the journey, his inadequate room, his appalling hunger, the awfulness of Beirut since they were there, his need for a huge drink.

Mrs Mark was the first to give up. 'Oh dear,' she said and stood back. 'I suppose we had better go in.'

'Oughtn't Adam to have a colossal drink first?' her husband broke in, blowing out his fleshy cheeks. But Andrew was standing quietly by the door and so they paraded in.

It was a large room. The windows were open onto the top lawn but the scent of gardenias, mixed with something marvellous to eat, rose from the candle-lit table. Portraits trembled in heavy gold frames. Adam sat on Mrs Mark's right with the petit-point woman on his right. He felt uncomfortable in his day clothes.

'I am sorry there are so many people.' Mrs Mark's voice was both musical and tired, like a handbell deadened with the touch of a hand. 'But we have the cricket match against the village tomorrow and, as we always lose, Ferdinand has recruited some maximum players.'

Staring about him, as Andrew placed something beneath his nose, Adam did notice a number of strong young men, red-faced and uncomfortable in their tight dinner-jackets, listening patiently to Mary.

'Oh dear, how disgusting.' Mrs Mark donned a pair of spectacles to examine what was before them. 'Asparagus. I'm so sorry about the food here, but we don't notice any longer. Some people bring their own and have it in their rooms. Jolly does.'

'Jolly? Jocelyn Ambrose?'

'The one. He's arriving after dinner. He has to be in England to have something done to him, poor fellow. Do you know him?'

'I had lunch at Rapallo. It didn't go very well.'

'Do tell.'

'Well,' said Adam, who had forgotten his day clothes. 'A girl arrived suddenly from England and I had to take her with me. Jolly refused to recognise her and kept calling her Adam as if she were just a bit of me.'

Mrs Mark laughed with her mouth open; but it was impossible not to listen to Mary. Although there were two dozen people at dinner, all particular conversation had subsided below her account of the night before. Adam wanted to change the subject.

Fortunately, Mrs Mark's thoughts were still with

Ambrose. 'You're very Arab, aren't you? I've put some things out in the library for you and Jolly to mull over, letters from Lady Anne Blunt, that sort of thing, very dull but the best we can do. Otherwise, he takes out the miniatures and writes all over them which annoys the other bods.'

At times, Adam found his hostess hard to follow as she kept up a concentrated conversation while attending to her left-hand neighbour, ensuring Mary did not cause trouble among the athletes and providing detail to her husband's stories miles away beyond the candelabra and gardenias.

'Poor Beirut,' she said suddenly in her muffled bell voice. 'We went there on a cruise. Billy was always missing the sailing as he kept finding wild flowers that made him faint. It all seemed to work then. What happened?'

'I don't think they ever liked one another much and then the Palestinians came in after being booted out of Jordan and sort of put the wind up the Christians who'd been top dogs up till then.' It was one of his better efforts.

'Yes. Poor things. They ought to have a place of their own. I know if I were booted out of this dump, I'd be no better than the PLOs, staying with my friends for weeks on end and breaking all their best things.' She had a way of laughing before, rather than after, a sentence. She looked into the darkness around her. 'Not that this place really belongs to us.'

Adam looked at her.

'Oh dear, we sort of squat here, you know. The dump belongs to the past, to the public, of course, and to cricketers and *Country Life* and God-like figures like Jolly. Come on ladies,' she said. They all got up. 'It's always been like that, from the beginning. Like living beside a museum.' She led the women out.

Once again, and through no effort of his own, Adam found himself in the place of honour as they arranged themselves around Mary's father. Mark's fleshy frame trembled as he pushed bottles of different liqueurs industriously round before him. Ferdinand and the athletes had started throwing bread. Adam's mind had emptied of conversation. He took his coffee.

'Why don't you take sugar?' Mark asked suspiciously, eyeing Adam from beneath heavy brows.

'It complicates things and the spoon rattles.'

'Oh but I do agree.' Mark's face relaxed into a smile of great warmth. 'Like an aspen. You, too. Malaria, I suppose. Near East?' He eyed Adam again. 'That is how you know Jocelyn Ambrose?'

'No.' An athlete now had a head-lock on Ferdinand. 'I went to . . .'

'He is here for a rather delicate operation. But I hear there is a bit of a to-do in his old office, as well.'

Ferdinand collapsed to the carpet with a splintering of chair wood and Mary's voice reached them through the darkness that Jolly had arrived, the old pederast.

'Hurry,' said Mark, rising quickly. 'Remember you are all on trial for the honour of my house.' He bolted for the door.

Jocelyn Ambrose had arrived but by the time Adam entered the drawing room, after a struggle of politeness with the athletes at the door, the old man had hardly penetrated the room. He moved with tiny steps as if he were wearing bedroom slippers too large for him, but his feet were shod in shiny half-brogues. He wore a brown tweed suit with an old fashioned ventless cut. Nothing marked him as a man who had turned his back on the manners and morals of his native country, as the greatest Orientalist of the age or as the arbiter of pre-war taste unless it was the spotted bow-tie that flourished over his waistcoat or the perfectly bald head. He wore round sun-glasses.

His progress round the room, led by both Mary and her mother, was slow for he stopped to speak to everybody, even the athletes' wives turning the pages of photograph albums.

'He has a bag, don't you know?' The words were hissed into Adam's ear. He spun round but only Mark was in his part of the room and he was examining with care a small bush on which a single mango was turning from green to yellow.

Adam felt a breath of misery. At Rapallo, he had admired the life dedicated to sunny, *pointilliste* learning and the

Moghul *douceur de vivre*. A single violet lay by each place and little birds flew out of the napkins and swarmed into a yellow cloud before the servants shooed them out into the garden with tall feather fans. Adam thought of the single *qasidah* of Mutanabbi, translated into the English of Dryden, the 'Glossary of Arabic words in the dialect of Palermo' and the little green-and-gold private edition of the 'Canon against the Koran', which he had been shown after lunch along with its illustrator, a young man from Munich with beautiful shirts. Then Adam thought of the colostomy and his eyes closed, for the first time since he had arrived at Helle.

'You know Adam Murray, don't you, you foolish old man?'

'I believe you came to us once, did you not? You brought a young woman with you, if I remember.' He spoke very softly, making the words only with the front of his mouth and smiling to accommodate them. Adam was embarrassed. 'She was, I believe, the daughter of the Archbishop of York.'

She was nothing of the sort, she was Laura, daughter of a man who divided his time without profit between Kent and the Hebrides, Laura Penrose, who had arrived without warning at Pisa aerodrome with 350 lire and £5 in silver. Adam had been forgiven.

'Rather a good-looking girl, if I remember,' Ambrose said as if to emphasize this point. 'Queen Ingrid was rather taken with her. We had to be very careful, didn't we?'

Mark slid between them like a torpedo. 'You're mad, Jocelyn, barking mad. You must have something to eat and an immense drink.'

'I have already quietly dined,' the old man said. 'I ate a light dinner in what I believe is called a lay-by. I no longer travel by railway train in England, William. In Italy, yes, if they are not striking. We must talk a bit more,' he said, turning back to Adam and smiling his unpleasant smile. 'It is some time since I had reliable word from Beirut.'

Mary had vanished and Ferdinand, without evident despair, was organising billiard fives for his guests. Adam said his goodnights – Ambrose's reply was particularly rich in suggestion – but on passing down gallery and passages already half-familiar, he found the outside door of Mary's room locked. He returned to his room puffing out his chest in deliciously pompous irritation, but it was with annoyance that he woke some time later to feel Mary pushing him sideways to make room in the bed. 'What are you doing?'

'I just want to see if we're a fit. You know, like in bridge,' she whispered loudly into his ear.

Adam burst out laughing until she put her mouth over his. Mary smelled of wool and soap. When she made love, she turned her head to the side and a distant look came into her eyes. This had troubled Adam at first but he had come to the conclusion that this was the look she thought was expected of her while making love, a rule of conduct, like the straight-back driving or no oysters in May and hare never, because they screamed so dreadfully when wounded.

'Thank you,' she said. 'Much better than chastity.'

'Ah, look, Mary. Was it true all that thing at dinner about David trying to screw you?'

She laughed out loud. 'You tried to take matters in hand when Toby passed out. You're so funny when you're drunk. You become a different person. You wander around with your hands behind your back like the Duke of Edinburgh. Poor Adam, I think you genuinely want to be respectable.' She kissed and then bit his shoulder. 'Poor old Adam, you're not made for the 80s.'

'What about you? Twenty-four people at dinner. I never heard such nonsense.'

'Well it won't last much longer.'

'But David? What about David?'

'I wouldn't worry about him.'

They slept until the housemaid pulled back the curtains on another brilliant Whitsun day. She did not seem to notice the extra hump in the bed for Mrs Hutchinson had been with the family all her working life and was, Mary explained from under the blankets, quite blind.

CHAPTER THREE

'Have you ever had a toothbrush break on you?' Mark was alone in the sunny breakfast room, standing and looking out over the top lawn and eating porridge at speed. From the disarray at the table and sideboard, it seemed that Ferdinand, the athletes and their wives had fed and left for the cricket pitch. Of Mary, there was no sign.

'No Sir.' Adam swallowed the sir.

'I have. This morning. Terrifying.' He set down his plate and bolted from the room.

Adam piled a plate high and gathered a sheaf of newspapers towards him. He had not progressed far with either when he looked up. The sun was hot through his last clean shirt and a pain had broken out in his side. He walked onto the terrace to smoke a luxurious cigarette. From a distance, he could hear the sound of batting and a brass band but the cigarette tasted thin. A second burned his mouth and he threw it into an urn. Adam wandered. In the drawing room, he sat down and looked at the photograph albums. Horses won races and young men, their stockings salmon pink and their faces bright from the sun, cradled open shotguns while women in tweed coats and skirts passed them things from the backs of wagons. A book caught his eye from the shelves, but he had hardly picked it out before he saw another with equal claims to interest. He examined a tall Gainsborough group and was intoxicated by the scent of greenhouse flowers. He turned to the arrangement on the table, culminating in a spectacular amaryllis, and saw a good carpet he could not quite identify. His side throbbed.

'Absurd,' said Adam out loud and remembered the letters waiting for him in the library. He set off with fixed purpose down the empty gallery crossed with sun. He found the library locked. He was just turning away, all purpose evaporated, when the door opened gently and Ambrose stood before him, dressed in a cream linen suit and with a small jeweller's glass attached to his sun-glasses.

'Come to admire the miniatures?' He turned and waddled back across the carpet which, Adam noticed, matched the ceiling plasterwork. The curtains were drawn against the sun and the light came from a row of ornate reading lamps hinged to the stacks.

'Aren't there some letters?'

'Molly has reluctantly allowed me the Timurid box from the safe.' He giggled and sat down at a little desk. 'I am afraid the attributions are in rather a tangle.'

Adam watched over the old man's shoulder as he passed the miniatures onto the open leaf of their case: three nobles picnicked beside a stream with deer and songbirds scattered among cypresses and pomegranate bushes; the Sultan dispensed justice before a rickety pavilion; a girl looked out from the balcony of a leaning tower. Each bore the little Helle mark, a sunburst.

'I saw your father at the Club,' Ambrose said without looking up from his flat, sunny world. He was writing little notes feverishly in the margin of a typewritten catalogue. Adam took a step closer. Against the entry for the girl, he had written: 'I'm afraid not. JA.' Their eyes crossed.

'I don't know why Molly has him any more. He has lost whatever judgment he had.' He giggled and looked up at Adam. 'Oh no. Oh no. Not your papa. Butterworth. I saw him at the club. I've resigned from the Athenaeum. I am told the ladies smoke cigars in the dining room.'

The next entries and the initials he simply scored out and wrote: 'Surely yes! JA.'

'He was rather concerned about your future.' Before the Sultan, a man was kneeling and the executioner's sword was raised. 'He said that mothers always warned their sons against certain families. Palmers, I think; Stanleys of Alderley; Marks, certainly. He seemed quite sure of it.'

'My father? My father said that?'

Ambrose looked up and detached his jeweller's glass. 'Do you know Mr Butterworth?'

'Isn't he at the Foreign Office?'

'No. Rather a nice little Jew. Thinks he knows about Islamic painting. Likes being beaten. By dark ladies. Has one in Bath, I am told. He was there. At lunch with your papa.' Ambrose began reorganising the miniatures into one pile. 'You became acquainted with the Palestinians, he said.'

Adam took a deep breath but Ambrose cut him off. 'You also know Sir Donald Penrose?'

'I was friendly with his son at Oxford. He was the best Arabic scholar they had had, oh, for years. And it was the daughter that Ex-Queen Ingrid . . .'

'Yes, yes,' Ambrose said impatiently. 'The boy is now in Beirut. He said. It's the Jews who ruined everything. Why couldn't they stay out of it?' Ambrose spoke with such venom that Adam took a step back. Then the old man relaxed and began moving the miniatures from one side of the box to the other, this time without the glass. 'I cannot say I am devoted to the Lebanese Christian politicians either. Mr Gemayel and his son came to lunch with us. I did not care for either of them. I asked them to give their guns to Bruno before lunch. They could have them back after lunch, you see. The son kissed the cook.'

'Who? Bachir?'

Ambrose giggled. 'Mr Butterworth thought he could use him. Foolish Mr Butterworth.' He giggled again and looked up at Adam. 'Wasn't there some incident with them last year? Some unpleasantness? A man was hit. He said.'

Adam wanted to sit down but Ambrose had taken the only chair and the library steps seemed somehow attached to the shelves. 'What do you mean? I don't quite understand?'

Ambrose was once again buried in the album. 'I rather liked Beirut. I was there in old St John Philby's day. Never knew Kim or that frightful woman. He was a traitor but St John was nice. Dirty, of course. Had an Arab mistress. Made mistakes speaking.'

'So do I. I can't say a sentence without a grammatical mistake.'

'He thinks you could do some good there. If you went back. You could go for a newspaper, couldn't you? Can't waste our youth in a parish of rich women, can we? And your clever friend is there.'

Adam felt sweat ruining his last clean shirt. He stepped back onto the carpet medallion which matched the ceiling's plaster sunburst. 'You think it would be a good idea for me to go back? Go back in the middle of all that?' Adam's voice squeaked a little as he spoke.

'Oh yes. Oh yes. It is a good opportunity. Many people find the atmosphere stimulating. The skin of civilization stripped away and what do we find? Only it's called something different from my day. Too many traitors.'

Ambrose rose with colossal slowness from his chair, closed the album and locked it in the desk. He took Adam's arm. 'I suppose we ought to join them outside. If you are to have any lunch.'

Sport made Adam anxious. He could not ride or jump, kill birds cleanly overhead, land a silver salmon trembling on the bank, stay in, win a set at tennis or play croquet without an irresistible temptation to cheat. He could, at least, console himself, in the course of their agonizingly slow progress across the park, that his arrival with Ambrose marked him out as a compensating intellectual while his known tenderness for Mary would preclude, even in the mind of the dullest athlete, the association of pederasty.

Once out in the hot sunlight, Adam regained his composure. As they walked, he thought back over their conversation and the mysterious *he*, who could be, who must be his father. It was simply another of George's schemes that spring to life, after lunch, in the smoking room of the Club, between tales of other men's good wars. Yet something troubled Adam, a word or a question which was like a hole, as if he had just lost or broken something that could not be replaced or repaired except at great cost. Ambrose was silent, concentrating on his tiny steps.

The scene that looked perfect from the park, the men in white on a green field, the brass band and the ladies floating before the pavilion, proved not so happy on their arrival. Mary was telling a story to a captive wife, but did not look up. Further off, Ferdinand and his father were walking up and down in great discomfort. Adam and Ambrose joined them.

'Our only hope is rain,' Ferdinand said, shaking his tousled hair and bouncing a cricket ball up and down on his bat. Adam looked up; the sky had lost some of the blue of breakfast time.

'Rain,' said his father, twitching his shoulders. 'Our only hope is rain.'

Ferdinand had not been able to lose the toss since Mary had spun the silver crown. It would have been folly to resist his team's clamour to exploit the perfect batting wicket. The first pair had proved all but unstoppable and despite an exemplary 1 from the captain at third and the quiet advice to his replacement, as they crossed, that 50 might not be a bad limit, the score had climbed in rapid slices of that amount. It now stood at 281 for five with each great stroke over the bowler's head or under the ladies' chairs greeted with a howl of pleasure from the pavilion and the slap of tin plates on the tally.

'Can't you declare, Ferdinand?' Adam asked.

Ferdinand shook his head vehemently and let fall the ball he was bouncing.

'Never happened,' said his father. 'Before lunch. Never before. Rain is our only hope.'

'Defeat might strengthen their sinews and bring them back hungry for revenge next year.' Ambrose had sat down and donned a Panama hat.

Mark and his son looked at the old man vaguely, the despair of victory in their eyes.

'Don't worry, our lot can have some smack,' Mary shouted up from where she was sitting. 'Adam's sure to have some.'

Adam looked at her.

'Oh shut up, Mary,' said Ferdinand quickly.

'What, my dear?'

'Palmers, Stanleys of Alderley,' Ambrose mused upwards into the heavy sky.

The ball careered into a pile of empty chairs by the tally. The umpires turned for the pavilion. Ferdinand walked out to meet his heroes as they returned, diffidently unstrapping their pads. Adam tried to catch Mary. He was, however, caught in the mill of people pushing, as politely as hunger would allow, into the lunch marquee and found himself, alone with Ferdinand of the house party, seated with the village team.

Eventually, the light through the white canvas diminished and Adam's neighbours became restless. Adam escaped to where Mary was sitting, with her mother and Ambrose, at the head of a table vacated by the home side.

'Oh Adam. Aren't you still hungry?' Mrs Mark made a place for him. 'Have some of Jolly's pills. Filling and much nicer.' Ambrose had arrayed a set of Battersea boxes and was showing their contents. Adam turned to Mary.

'Shouldn't Adam play as he's staying?' Mary's mouth was tight shut.

'Why should he? People must do what they like. I know what, Mare, Adam.' Her smile embraced them both. 'Why don't you give Adam your tour of the pictures. Jolly would only write all over them, wouldn't you, you foolish old man?'

Ambrose smiled as Mrs Mark detached from her belt a large bunch of keys. Mary whisked them up from the table and set off through the marquee, her skirt with its inch of visible petticoat swinging against her long legs.

Adam had difficulty catching up with her as she strode across the park towards the house. As he increased his speed, so, it seemed, did she and he was forced to launch his question from several yards behind.

'Why did you say that?'

'Say what, my Arafat?' Mary looked over her shoulder and slowed down.

'About me and smack.'

'I wouldn't worry about that. I'll show you the greenhouses first. They're rather sad but Dad built them after Sweet Nothing won the Prix de l'Arc.'

They reached a walled garden, with rows of espaliered peach trees held back by wire, and, turning its corner,

31

came on the greenhouse. Mary fumbled through the keys.

'Why did you deliberately embarrass me?'

Mary pulled the door open and they were passing down a gravel path between ranks of red geraniums and carnations while a huge plumbago trailed blue flowers from the roof.

'Dad loves scented pelargoniums. Here, smell.' She took Adam's hand to rub the furry leaf.

He looked up to speak but she was opening another door, steamed with condensation, onto a copse of small fruit trees, lemons, oranges, and the tree that carries both fruit. The smell stung Adam's senses and something dripped on him from above.

'Mary, you must answer me.' She was now at another door into another, steaming room, where plantains overhung a little pond spread with lilies. Beyond were pawpaws and trees Adam had never seen, with ripe orchids tumbling from mossy nests on their trunks. The air was so wet and heavy, Adam could scarcely breathe.

'Mary. Please tell me what you are trying to do.'

She turned on him. 'Oh, don't be so pompous. Who cares what they think? Why do you want to be like them?'

'You're mad,' said Adam wearily and sat down on a stack of bricks.

Mary took a step forward and slapped him across the cheek and, at the instant of her touching him, he felt all his strength run out of him. Adam burst into tears.

She stared at him in horror.

'You don't have to cry, you know, Adam.'

'Yes, I know.' Adam wiped his eyes on his dripping sleeve.

'Come and have some nice brandy and you'll feel better.' She took his arm and led him out into the air.

At the malachite drinks table outside the drawing room, they each drank a large brandy and then another.

'Have one of these.' She handed him a little pill. 'I stole them off Jolly. Perhaps they'll make us a bit nicer to each other.'

'Jolly thinks I ought to go back to Beirut.' He swallowed the pill. His heart was fluttering with the brandy.

'Jolly really means he wants you to go down on him.'

'I'm not going to. Go back I mean. He's a terrific anti-semite.'

'Of course you're not. Let's go and see the attics. Bring your drink.'

'What about the pictures?' Adam said as they walked down the gallery.

'I wouldn't worry about them. Anyway, the public are there.'

'For someone who knows so much about pictures,' he said, keeping step with her, 'you avoid them like the plague.'

'Oh, Adam, don't be a bore. This isn't a museum. They're nothing to do with us any more, can't you see?'

The house diminished in comfort as they climbed until, on the last floor, there was only a bare passage lit by naked bulbs. In place of carpets, there was a sprinkling of dead flies. On the walls were dirty prints of the house or of dead game or an occasional lifeless family group – the children in smocks gathered round some sombre matriarch on the double staircase while young men with moustaches leaned easily against the urns, offering their profiles to the photograph. As they walked round the dome, Adam saw that angels and clouds had dropped great flakes of paint and plaster.

The rooms were not empty. Grey light leaked through the *oeil de boeuf* windows on bedroom chairs stacked to the ceiling or rows of brass bedsteads. Occasionally, a cot or a basin and a jug grey with dust gave evidence of former occupation, as in a defunct prison.

'It must be further down.' But the next room was lamps, white and lathe-turned, and the next underfelt and then ink-stands, bath-boards, clothes-horses, curtains, trouser-presses. Each time Adam emerged, Mary would be down the passage, beckoning. At last Mary opened a door and stopped. To Adam, the room seemed just like the others, only there were feather mattresses folded in heavy rolls around the walls. In a small clearing in the middle stood a rocking-horse and a model of the house. A bluebottle was dying noisily on the window-ledge.

'I haven't been up here for years.' Mary stood in the

middle of the room and breathed deeply. 'I used to come up here all the time. Once I spent a whole day and night up here and Billy went and rang the police and they all went through the park in a line. I saw them from up here, beating with sticks like at a shoot.'

The dolls' house was hinged at the side. Adam kneeled down and prised it open into two equal halves, releasing an old smell of nurseries.

'Old Mr Sisley in the Department of Works made it for me when I was in hospital.'

The wood was worked and varnished but the windows had been pierced and some of the gilded roof urns were missing or leaned at angles. Adam found the dining room, where tiny footmen were ranged against the walls. They had been twisted into curious postures or lacked arms or legs. In the library, where Adam had spoken to Ambrose, painted carpet matched painted ceiling but the leather backs of the tiny books had been picked off one by one. The floor of the drawing room had come away from its walls and the table under the conversation piece, with its bouquet culminating in a spectacular silk lily, was slipping off. Adam tried to steady it.

'I was a destructive child.'

Adam looked at her curiously. She had leaned back against the stack of mattresses and was staring at him, her mouth half-open. House martins were shrieking in the eaves above the oval window. Adam felt hot and covered with dust. Mary began to roll up her dress and petticoat. Adam took a step towards her.

'You're quite pretty, you know.'

'Thank you.'

Dust filled Adam's nose and mouth. Under his fingers, he could feel small grains of dust against Mary's skin and dress. He tasted grit on the inside of her lips. The house martins stopped their racket. The fly was dead. Adam followed the stripes of the ticking, deep blue on dirty cream, running this way and that as far as his eyes could focus. Sweat filled his eye-sockets.

'You do rather love it, don't you, poor thing?' Mary pushed Adam gently aside.

'But don't you?' Adam thought his face must be red.

'I do if you do, my Caliph.' She got up and smoothed down her dress.

'It's raining,' she said suddenly. Adam looked up and the oval pane was streaked with rain.

From deep down, in the courtyard of the house, Adam heard scurrying footsteps and the clatter of studs on cobbles. A voice was raised in triumph and delight, Mary's father's, repeating over and over again: 'A draw. A very palpable draw.'

Adam was dressing in his room when he heard a knock at the door. In fact, he was not dressing but staring in disgust at the shirt laid out limply on the back of the chair, so smelly and creased and unlike the lawn sheets or the white towels hanging on the clothes horse. He opened the door to Mrs Hutchinson, who crossed the room with confident steps and deposited a pile of ironed shirts on the dressing-table.

'Oh, Mrs Hutchinson. You've saved my life.'

'The girl did them,' she said in her country voice and turned about as if even sightless eyes could pick out any disorder in one of the rooms under her charge. 'I thought you wouldn't want to be wearing the same shirt all day.

Adam picked up a shirt, still warm from the iron, but Mrs Hutchinson stood stockily in the middle of the room. She showed no inclination to leave.

'A real terror, that Miss Mary, though you have to love her for it.' Adam was aghast at this expression of opinion but the old woman was smiling to herself and hurried on. 'She used to ride her pony all over the park, jumping anything she came to, it did my husband so proud to see her though he's gone now.'

Adam stood buttoning his shirt.

'Mrs Hutchinson . . .' he began but she was standing still in the middle of the room, the smile drifting off her mouth.

'It almost broke his heart to kill the pony though William helped, the one who was here before that Andrew.'

'But what happened? When was this?'

'She was in Exeter General all those weeks and this specialist came down from town. Mrs Mark stayed with her day and night. We had to do an extra room for this Dr

Smale.' Her blind eyes roved the room and fixed at last on the window.

'He gave her injections all the time. All the time. You see, they thought she might wake up. Oh yes, she had all those injections.'

All that Sunday it rained at Helle. Soon after breakfast, the athletes became restless, their task completed if not crowned with success, and they gathered up their females and BMWs and left. Ferdinand politely left with them. Even Ambrose was tucked gently into the back of his large vehicle and borne off to London Airport and home; although not before he had promised to put something in Adam's way that might help with the book.

They lunched dully together, the four who remained, at a small round table erected specially in the dining-room. The Marks, for some reason, ate only boiled rice and drank water. The talk was of Toby, his unpredictable conduct, his need for employment.

'Can't you do something for him, Billy,' Mrs Mark cried out. 'Why can't people see his point?'

'A delightful person with many talents, my dear,' was her husband's reply.

'What became of the bank and Paris?'

'Oh, you know how it is,' said Mary glumly, but did not add that Toby now worked in Harrods.

After lunch, she again disappeared. Although Adam felt better than he had on Saturday, he felt drawn to the drinks table with its array of bottles. He went downstairs to look at the picture. By daylight, even the weak daylight of that wet Sunday, the resemblances were not so marked. The cupid in the laurel had lost the smile he remembered from Brightwell and the lady's arm was thrown back in a beckoning gesture while a strand of drapery looked after her modesty.

'Mary thinks it is Sir Joshua.' Mark's appearance startled Adam. 'But we fear the scorn of Jocelyn.' He turned to reveal a lighted doorway from which, Adam presumed, he had just emerged. 'It's not just the bum, don't you know?

He's come back. The new man has turned out to be a busted flush.' He cocked his head to the unmistakable clatter of Mary's heels on the marble staircase. 'Something to do with the Near East.' He braced himself for Mary's appearance.

'Oh, hello, Dad,' she said suspiciously. 'Come on Adam. We must leave if we're to get back to London.'

The suitcases had been packed and were already piled in the hall. Andrew was transferring them to Mary's car. Adam said his thanks but his pockets ached and he felt a twinge of guilt in shaking hands with Andrew. The butler, however, made a small fist of his hand and put it directly in his coat pocket.

On the way back, Adam resolutely stayed awake although, once beyond Helle, the world was ugly. They seemed to be driving through perpetual town, travelling not on highways but streets, with roundabouts and traffic lights and suburban houses as in a child's reading-book. In starved copses by the roadside, men waited. Adam rested his head in Mary's lap to shut the world out.

'I'll tell you something about Jolly,' she said at length. 'He's a junkie.'

Adam banged his head against the steering-wheel. 'Are you mad?' Outside was a chaos of flyovers and motorway sliproads.

'Guess what Mrs Hutchinson found in his room.' She gestured to her bag which lay at Adam's feet.

He reached into it and drew out the largest object in it, a case of glass and shiny metal. It contained a syringe, heavy and balanced like a weapon.

'Jolly's little helper,' Mary said excitedly and reached out to touch the case. Adam opened it. He examined the metal shaft with its glass window graded for the dose and the heavy brass thumbpiece. He touched the end of the needle and found it quite blunt.

'Oh Mary, it's probably something to do with his bottom. You don't want this.' Adam rolled down his window on the motorway skipping below them.

'Don't you dare.' With her free hand, she snatched it from him and dropped it at her side. 'We'll leave it behind the sofa cushions at home. That will give those cricketers something

37

to think about.' She began to laugh and drew Adam towards her.

They arrived at Clements Street to find Toby and Laura had quarrelled. Laura at first refused to say anything but Mary stood on her authority as householder. Toby, it seemed, had pushed Laura down the stairs and she had bruised her arm, not very badly. He had since vanished, Oates-like, into a glistening Chelsea.

More surprising was the presence of Oliver, who was standing by the gramophone, smiling and smoothing the strands of hair across his bald spot, swaying gently to records Adam had not known the house possessed.

CHAPTER FOUR

Adam rarely felt alone. Since childhood, he had performed before watchers, not angels but spectators deathless and English, had sensed their ghostly approbation as he felt he was going forward, had thought to hear soft intakes of breath as he turned into an alley and saw the whitewashed wall at its end. His sisters had religion, George Murray and Mary had Rules of Conduct, little ordinances of pronunciation or diet that are the moraine left by a society that has lost its nerve and slipped. Adam had his watchers.

'The Palestine Liberation Organisation is facing its greatest challenge,' he typed. 'The next three months will show if it can survive as an independent political and military force.' Adam looked up. The ghostly gallery, attentive and disapproving, melted into an audience a month away, a scattering of diplomats and journalists and scholars and, perhaps, a retired soldier or two, gathered by Ambrose to hear this first condensation of Adam's book. It was not a very good first sentence.

Adam listened for a moment to the sounds from the mews, the homosexual couples on either side, re-arranging perfect households, and chauffeurs slapping water on the roofs of large black cars. Mary was at a sale-room looking at picture frames, as she would say. Adam tried again: 'Nobody here would wish to die for émigré bureaucracy, so ossified and so divided that no action is possible but incompetent violence. Yet the Palestine Liberation Organisation . . .'

Adam stood up and lit a cigarette. If only Johnny were in London, he thought. Johnny had a way of clearing his head. Once, the first year, as they were turning onto the Corniche just before the Lunapark, Johnny had stopped and said,

'Can't you feel it, the whole sea wall crumbling', and Adam had walked to the edge and seen large rats scurrying among the sandstone reefs. Even then, even before the Civil War and the Kataib massacres of Palestinians and the Palestinian massacres of Christians, Johnny never thought of being impartial. No good to either side, he would say; not trusted by either side; just make clear where you stand and where you belong.

There was no doubt to which side Johnny belonged. That shock of red hair, the boyish face, the slow, easy walk. Johnny was at home in that vicious, infantile, chivalrous city even on days when the police dared not go about. He knew the militias, even those created overnight by some Arab régime to fight its incomprehensible struggle for influence in the only free city in the world. Johnny was a West Beirut man. In the eastern suburbs or among the beach cabins of Jounieh with Marcel or Max or Pierre in their neat Israeli cast-off uniforms, Johnny was unimaginable.

Yet how slowly it had crumbled! That Sunday last year, when they shelled the beaches from Jounieh and Adam had gone straight from the hospital and was sick in the university garden, even the students under the pines were quiet, the whole city was quiet, thinking: the children, no, not on the beaches, no, not on a Sunday, no, that is not what was intended, no, it is the situation.

But the city went on. The Riviera Club reopened and every day something occurred, a piece crumbled away, a hand grenade was thrown into an Emergency Room, a car bomb devastated a school, and the whole city was silent a moment, on both sides of the Green Line, east and west, thinking: the hospital, no, the school no, this is not what was intended, it is the situation.

It was no good. There was too much evidence of his friends around him: a glass half-full of whisky, a torn silk stocking, contact prints of Laura's face for a magazine. 'Absurd,' said Adam out loud and scratched himself.

One of his least favourite tasks at Clements Street, unnoticed and self-imposed, was to gather up the post before it piled too high inside the front door and to sort out those bills that had to be paid. Toby and he never received official

40

letters, Mary never opened them, and the telephone had twice been disconnected and, once, the water.

Adam put aside Mary's parking tickets which he might present gently like some confidential agent or the Comptroller at Helle or he might ignore since they were not really his affair. While sifting through the other bills, he came to his surprise on the old-fashioned handwriting of his father.

The letter was addressed to Adam care of Lydia, his sister in Malmesbury, for George Murray did not recognize Clements Street. It skimmed effortlessly and legibly over a succession of small family matters before alighting, in its last paragraph, on an invitation to lunch to meet a Mr Butterworth of the Foreign Office. Adam was already framing an excuse, effortless and legible, when he glanced at the postmark or rather the two postmarks. Cursing Lydia's slowness, he ran upstairs and pulled a disintegrating tie from the chaos of Toby's things in Laura's room.

St James's Park was sunny and early secretaries were lying on the grass beside their tiny lunches of yoghurt and cheesecake. Adam looked at them sourly. Yet descending into the small, subterranean club bar, he found George Murray alone. In a grey suit, clutching a grey drink against the luxuriant Morris paper, he looked like an elf in long grass.

'Adam, old fellow,' he said, taking him warmly by the hand. 'Have a nice drink. They make good Tom Collinses here.'

The barman smiled in acknowledgment. George Murray smiled too, but as if he understood a little of the meaning of the world, the virtue of a cool, strong drink on a hot day, a spot of luncheon to put something in the way of his boy, undisturbed by the furious *canaille*. George Murray had devoted his life to selling steel pipes to the Middle East and Eastern Europe, but he had not lost his love of beauty or of the great world, and though he had often heard the chimes at midnight, he could name the clockmaker and the clock.

'That would be nice. I don't think I have met Mr Butterworth, have I?'

'He has quite turned the club around. We are on the

Finance Committee together and he proposed some unpopular measures which I felt bound to support. He has retired from the office, now, but keeps very much in touch.' George Murray's voice dropped in respect, then he twinkled one of his eyes. 'Likes *cioccolata*. Looks like a dog biscuit.'

They both straightened up as an immense figure strode through the door, wearing some regimental tie or other and a brownish suit. Above suit and tie, something seemed to go wrong. The face was dry and patterned with little freckles and the hair on the crown and upper lip seemed weedy and ill-nourished as if the air at that great height was too thin to support it. George Murray recoiled at his ugliness.

'Ah yes,' said Butterworth briskly, as George Murray gathered himself and introduced Adam. 'I am looking forward to your paper at Bath. I will be chairing that session in place of Ambrose to ensure it does not get rowdy. I'm afraid Jocelyn Ambrose must recognise that he is getting badly out of touch.' He refused a drink and the Murrays, with regret on the one hand and anxiety on the other, drained their glasses and followed him upstairs.

'I hope you're enjoying the research,' Butterworth said as they walked down the hall. 'A most interesting topic, the balance between political and military action. At the heart of all diplomacy.'

'I am,' said Adam. 'Though I sometimes find it hard to keep my distance.'

'Ah,' said Butterworth, and he stopped to glance at the Reuters tape. 'One needs a line in addition to one's regular activity. To keep everything in balance. Something more than the (you know German, of course) *Alltagstrott*.'

'*Mag sein*,' said Adam foolishly.

'I'm a businessman mostly now,' Butterworth said, turning to the dining-room and drawing out his notecase. 'Too many old fellows like me at the Office.' His card showed a company called Executive Resources Ltd and an address in Bruton Street.

'Head-hunting is the game now, wouldn't you say, Murray,' he said as Adam's father fumbled about a table. They found one by the window. Adam regretted his filthy tie but felt comfortable in the sunny room amid the matt linen and glass, the dirty pictures and chandeliers. Trust George to produce this character, he thought.

'We have a good new system,' George Murray said hurriedly. 'As one of the Committee's economy measures, we do not take hot food at luncheon and wine is bought for cash and by the glass.' Adam's heart sank as he queued and then piled his plate with indistinguishable pieces of pie before a number of apologetic matrons who had somehow escaped the Butterworth axe.

'Only way, I'm afraid,' said Butterworth and launched a crisp account of the crisis in the club, and his measures to overcome it; the sale of the wine-cellar which George had built up to the third best in London, the disposal of a Sargent group George had bought for nothing in Manchester, the admission of women to certain uncomfortable and badly-heated parts of the building. There was no temptation to linger over their plates and soon both Murrays were keen to smoke. This was not permitted.

'Sir Donald Penrose was in here the other day,' Butterworth said suddenly.

'An exceptional public servant,' said George Murray, twinkling. 'We got stuck together in Algiers in '56 when he was Undersecretary and we couldn't leave the Residence. While the mob went about its business, I composed a verse comedy and he designed . . .'

'He said that you were together with his son at Oxford.' Butterworth's brusque interruption left George Murray crestfallen but he did not seem to notice. 'Not that that is any recommendation. That Arabic school at Oxford should be reformed root and branch. It is now quite clear that Ambrose's influence on Arabic scholarship has been less than helpful, to say the least. Root and branch,' he repeated, staring at Adam. George Murray was twinkling at the matrons, perhaps for more glasses of wine.

'How well do you really know Beirut?' Butterworth said suddenly, but in Arabic. He spoke carefully, using the full classical forms and their endings.

'By God, not at all. I mean yes. I was there on a visit before the civil war and then for a short time just now.'

43

The sun was on Adam's back and he shifted his chair.

George Murray was looking at them both, pleased with this show of gentlemanly virtuosity. The matron brought not only two glasses of wine but also a heavy trifle. Butterworth tucked in and looked back at Adam.

'Although your first interest was the Palestinians, yet did you spend much time with the Kataib of Sheikh Bachir?'

'No. I mean it was not important. I made one large article about them after leaving the city and visiting their fighters on their side of the Green Line. I did not see Sheikh Bachir.' Adam wondered if he could take off his coat.

'You should have taken more care on the Green Line. You knew Mr Lukomski.'

'Yes. American.' Adam broke back into English. 'Roman Catholic. Had been in the Special Forces in Vietnam and never let you forget it.' Adam slowed down. 'I mean I only met him once. He was always handling weapons, too, which Bachir's men liked but I don't think is really on for journalists, even one of his sort.' Adam looked up at Butterworth insolently.

'Oh I do so agree,' said George Murray. 'In Rhodesia . . .'

'That was not the reason,' Butterworth interrupted again, his Arabic so careful and clear, 'for Lukomski's death. Your conduct, my boy, was at best foolishness. At best.'

'It was an accident, by God, you must understand.' Adam wanted to stand up.

'Perhaps. Ah Murray,' he said, reverting to English. 'I interrupted you but it is the language of all languages which no foreigner can learn. There are, of course, mistakes but young Murray is coming along quite nicely.'

That was that. Butterworth stood up, pleading business and looking forward to a valuable conference at Bath. The Murrays had no such business and, setting up in the smoking room, they all but completed a decanter of Club Special Port and a packet of high-tar cigarettes.

'I see this is also the scratching room. Very half-gentleman, Adam.'

'I'm sorry.'

44

But George Murray leaned back and looked up at the cut-glass chandelier, muttering to himself: 'Cold luncheon, cold luncheon.'

They were friends. After so much Club Special Port, their minds had settled on old-fashioned values, not on the brisk virtues of Mr Butterworth, who was a dry, old stick, pretending to keep up to date but when had George Murray ever heard Sir Donald mention him? Sir Donald . . .

As for George Murray's objections to the Clements Street arrangement, which were certainly not of principle but strong enough to have pressed him to arrange this lunch, these had faded before the horror of wine by the glass.

Adam deflected the only question about Mary, by mentioning the similarity of the two supposed Sir Joshuas, and this suggestion of parity brought to George Murray's mind the pleasant memory of correspondence with Billy Mark, during which they agreed that there was no original and no copy. The master had been looking for something, had painted the lady's head at Brightwell and bits and pieces at Helle ('More bits than pieces, I fear') but stopped, disappointed or distracted by another commission, and his students had done up both pictures for a few guineas, brushes and tallow.

Adam felt reassured as he tumbled down the steps into Pall Mall. It was only George, dear fellow, who had set this business in train. As for Butterworth, Adam thought as he walked across the park, what did he know about the Green Line? What the hell?

But Adam could not return to his work. He wandered the house all afternoon, draining glasses, until Toby's return from Harrods, simultaneously with the girls.

'Ah Toby. Can I have a word with you in private?' he said as Toby struggled to remove something bulky from his tight suit trousers. Mary and Laura stopped reviewing their day and joined them.

'Well, I suppose it concerns you all.' Adam was surprised to see Toby undo his flies. 'It's about Johnny. Do we know exactly where he is?'

'Got you,' said Toby, standing upright and flourishing

a tin. 'Pâté de foie gras truffé. Quite reasonable or not?'

The girls fell on the tin. 'Let's get some people round,' said Mary. 'We can have Adam's ducks hanging in the garage if darling will pluck them, won't you, my Sultan?'

'Look Mary, you're mad,' said Adam, anxious to get back to his point. 'Those ducks have been hanging there since before I arrived. I'm not sure they'll be edible.'

'Toby will make one his sauces. Don't be so lazy. You're always claiming to be adept at country pursuits. You bravely shot them, you must draw them and pluck them.'

'I did not shoot them. I don't know how to shoot. I was in Beirut.'

Toby was now doing up his flies. 'Come on, Adam. To the garage. I'll gralloch, you pluck.'

The garage was lined with trunks of Toby's old clothes and books which he had not the energy either to preserve or throw away. It smelled unpleasant.

'Did he say anything, Johnny, I mean? That night at Catford?'

Toby was gingerly handling the birds which hung from a roof beam. Feathers began to fall as he stroked their breasts. 'He banged on in the usual way. You know what he's like when he's plastered. Why?'

'I don't know. Can't you remember? You said something about dark hints.'

'What was it? Yes. Palestine is a state of mind. That was it. He said it a couple of times. Bloody stupid.'

'Bloody stupid. Any names? Did he mention any names? Lukomski, perhaps.'

Toby looked up. 'Wasn't he the go-between between the Christians and the Palestinians? It's all so complicated.'

'Toby, how do you know that? Who told you that? Did Johnny say that?'

'God knows. Probably read it somewhere. All shits as far as I'm concerned. I'm told the way to see if they're ready is to press the stomach and inhale what comes out of the beak. It ought to be a bit gamey but not too much. Are you ready?'

Adam picked up the limp head of the hen and then dropped it. He choked up filth, cigarettes and Club Special

Port. 'Throw them away.' Tears were streaming down onto his lips.

Toby looked hurt. 'I suppose you're right. Pity, though.' He placed the two birds reverently in the overflowing dustbin.

Mary's heart was set on duck. She drove off to buy another brace from a late shop, drawn, plucked and frozen, and they had quite a reasonable evening. David came with bottles of sweet champagne, making a great fuss of Mary and laughing politely at Toby's abuse. David proposed to Mary that they go on to Harry's night club and Adam was obliged to follow to keep an eye on them; even Toby, who was not popular with Harry's proprietor, risked an insolent entry with Laura under David's protection.

Yet the evening ended in the way that many evenings seemed to end, with Oliver appearing just as they began to think of him. Hours later, Adam would wake from his liquid sleep to find himself fully clothed on the bed with Mary and Laura, while Toby paced the floor.

Adam found Toby pacing slowly round in a circle, his hands behind his back.

'That's it. Thank you, God.' Toby tore his betting ticket in half and let it flutter to the ground where it joined a million others littering the concrete of Tattersall's. It was the Friday of Ascot Week and they had driven up from Kent. Adam's morning-coat was too tight and the top hat he had borrowed from Laura's father too large. Toby had failed to apply for a voucher for the Enclosure and looked cooler in his usual crumpled suit; but he was barred from all his friends but those who sought him out.

'Look, Toby. There's still the Windsor Castle. You know, I've got an account now.'

'No, no.' Toby went back to pacing in a circle, peering at Adam every now and then. 'Account, eh? Since when have we had an account? I assume it's in the tart's name.'

'No, it isn't. Since the Derby. Ferdinand arranged it.'

'Well, I've got £9 left.' Toby looked up insolently at the couples walking up and down in the Enclosure, the ladies holding their light hats in place though there was scarcely a breeze. Then he rounded on Adam: 'What are we doing? I mean it's all right for you. You have Mary to run your life and then there's the lecture on the Palestinians. 250 quid just for sucking up to Jolly. At least you're doing something. Look at me. Harrod's Food Halls!' He bellowed with laughter.

'You have Laura.'

'Have I?' Toby paced again. 'Laura is so vague I don't think she even notices when I interfere with her.'

Adam felt a fence at his back, dividing the Enclosure from Tattersall's, his morning-coat from Toby's crumpled suit. The bulldogs at the wicket gate wore bowler hats but were firm. 'Come on, I can't do any work at Clements Street, so what's the point? All those tarts and always being smacked out. I mean at Oxford, we all went about and Johnny and tons to drink and tripping every now and then. At times, we felt like heroes, there were so many possible futures. Now I sometimes wonder why I do one thing rather than another; each seems equally futile. At least with you, we get all that delicious food.'

Toby had expanded his operations: a York ham, a side of smoked salmon, gulls' eggs, even a 7-oz tin of Beluga caviar. Mary had bought several cases of drink and for a while now Toby had presided over the most elegant of dinners. 'I know I'll get caught,' he said. 'It just has to happen.' He turned and walked away from Adam.

'I'll put something on for you,' Adam shouted after him and then made his way back through the crowd to the Enclosure side of the paddock. Adam was on his own. Mary had disappeared immediately to a place she alone, as daughter of the chief steward, was permitted. Laura was escorting her father. David was entertaining strangers.

The two-year-olds were already parading round the paddock ring when Adam pushed through to the rail. He made out Laura, holding her father tightly by the arm. She had trodden down the backs of her shoes and her left stocking was holed at the heel.

'Adam,' she said, making room for him. 'Are you going to make a bet?'

'Yes. I rather like the French horse, Riverrun. Which is he?' He looked down at his Timeform. 'No. 9. Ch. c.' No. 9 carried a green and red silk blanket and stepped carefully in and out of the shade of the broad lime trees, his head erect and alert, his coat a deep chestnut gloss.

'Ah yes, the Aga's.' Sir Donald Penrose looked sad and stern in his dark morning-coat. 'Played up rather last time out, Mr Bull says. I saw Boutin who said he had travelled well. Probably lying like all Frenchmen and trainers.'

Adam excused himself and pushed through the packed ranks at the paddock. He broke into a run. Amid the genial, hot throng, he heard the jockeys called to mount and then counted off as they cantered the runners past the stand. Adam reached the Tattersall's rails but could not find old Crowley. His son, in huge square checks, and a bald scribe, were taking the book.

'£50 on Riverrun, please. To win.'

Jim Crowley looked straight over Adam's head. 'Well, Mr Murray, we haven't yet had your settlement from Epsom, have we?' He looked down at Adam and smiled. 'Or should we send the account direct to the chief steward?' He nudged the scribe, who laughed into the book.

'I'll lay you nines on Riverrun.'

Adam spun round. A young man had leaned onto the rails. He had a pleasant open face and wore, of all things even for Tattersall's, a safari suit. His hair was so short, he looked like a soldier. He seemed a little drunk.

'Watch it, lad.' Old Crowley appeared suddenly over his son's shoulder, breaking off a tic-tac dialogue. 'Murray. About Riverrun, was it? 500 for 50. Thank you.' The scribe reluctantly wrote the bet down and Jim Crowley wiped the odds off his black-board. The boy in the safari suit had vanished.

Return was harder. The lawn was packed with people craning to see the start. Adam pushed himself through, scarcely knowing where he was headed, until he caught sight of Laura, still firmly holding her father but staring out towards the stand.

'Ah, there you are,' she said as Adam divided the last couple and reached her.

'Riverrun has broken down,' her father said, lowering his race-glasses. Adam squinted out over the heads. The runners had broken into two groups and, in the second of the two, moving easily, were the green-and-red silks. As they rounded the bend, Paquet urged the colt gently forward along the rails.

'Shout,' said Adam and gripped Laura's arm; and shout she did, and went on shouting as Paquet found a hole, caught the leader just opposite them and held him to the line.

'Did we win? Adam, I can't see. Did we win?'

'Oh yes, we won.'

'I'm afraid there'll be an inquiry,' Sir Donald said, gently, wrapping the cord around his race-glasses. 'It was as I expected. Paquet clearly took Piggott's ground.' He looked at Adam with triumph. 'And Billy Mark is chief steward.'

Adam could hear the bookies laying odds against an inquiry.

'Don't be silly, Papa,' Laura said, grasping her father now. As she spoke, the No. 9 plate ran up the finishing post scoreboard with a clank. 'How much did you have on?'

'Ten ponies,' Sir Donald said vaguely. 'Five for me; five for Mrs Eggins. But I doubt the Tote were even giving odds.' He raised his arm in a gesture of irreversible farewell and made for the stand.

Adam and Laura found themselves alone on the lawn.

'That will cheer him up for the whole weekend,' she said as she watched her father cross the line of shade into the stand tunnel. 'Why do you grind your teeth when you watch?'

'Do I?' Adam put his hand to his mouth. 'I suppose we had better find David and the others to celebrate.'

'Don't let's. I can't stand Oddjob's tart. Why do they all want to do it with him? Let's find Toby.'

Lawn gave way to concrete, morning-coats to suits, champagne to gin-and-tonic and then to litter, shirtsleeves and beer. But neither in Tattersall's, nor the Silver Ring, was Toby to be found. Laura collapsed onto a bench and took off her shoes.

'Poor Toby. I'm so worried about him,' she said as Adam

plumped down beside her. She looked closely at him and her eyes brimmed with tears. 'How will it all end? It can't go on, can it?'

Adam looked down at her bare arms, one of which still bore the bruise from her fall downstairs. 'Deaths and weddings. Isn't that the way they do it in books?'

'Adam, be serious. Sometimes I think I should have stayed at home with Papa.' She looked round blindly at the concrete and the litter and the men trying to walk straight. 'No Toby and no disgusting Oddjob.'

'Come on, Log, don't you start getting soppy about chastity.'

'She wore such lovely hats, at Ascot, my mother.' She stopped suddenly. The young man in the safari suit stood some distance away, staring at them and swaying, curiously aggressive and vulnerable. Adam took off his top hat to forestall comment.

'Look at me, Adam.' Adam looked down at her bruised arm. 'Don't take any notice. It's that horrid man who forced Johnny to sell his dog.' Adam kept his eyes down but felt the young man move on. 'He asked me to go with him,' she said in a whisper. 'Johnny, I mean.'

'Are you mad?' The young man had vanished.

'Of course not, but you know what Johnny's like. I couldn't. Papa is all alone now, but for the spaniels and Mrs Eggins.' Laura was trembling slightly. 'What do you think will happen? Papa was so pleased when he went in for the Foreign Office. Johnny did an interview and it all seemed to go quite well but that was it.' She paused for breath and turned her empty blue eyes on Adam. 'What is this Palestine Institute anyway?'

'Palestine Research Institute.' Adam knew it quite well. It was off Rue Verdun and he had spent some time there talking with its director, a gentle and mysterious man called Hussein Sarabi, who had lost his face to a parcel bomb. His hands were gone, too, but he would stand when Adam was ushered in so that Adam always extended his own hand till he touched, with revulsion, the smooth, pale forearm. They said Sarabi had twice recaptured the Holiday Inn from the Kataib but Adam had never seen him in uniform. His

Hebrew must have been good for he kept jotting things down off the radio, which was tuned to Kol Israel. 'Oh, they publish papers on conditions in the refugee camps. They're very bureaucratic now, the PLO.'

'What? He's with the terrorists?'

'Well, they aren't all terrorists. Some people think none of them is. It's just they haven't got a place of their own to fight in.'

'Adam, do be sensible. What's going to happen? It's all so complicated.'

'You know there's a sort of ceasefire with the Israelis. It's never completely quiet because of the shelling over the Green Line, but where Johnny is is well back.' Adam felt he was not getting across. 'You know, the Christian fighters, the Kataib or the Phalangists as some people call them, against practically everybody else but mostly the Palestinians and the Syrians'. Adam gave up and looked away. 'Johnny's Arabic is so good he can look after himself better than anyone I know.'

Laura seemed unsatisfied.

'Johnny will be all right. I might go back. I mean, when the book's done. I can't before that.' He got up. 'Let's go and join the others in the Enclosure.' He took her bruised arm and raised her lightly from the bench.

'Did you make a lot of money on Riverrun?'

'A bit. Not as much as your father.' He put his arm through hers and then removed it.

She stopped and blocked his way. 'You mustn't spend it on that stuff.'

'Then why on earth did you ask Oddjob to stay?'

'I didn't really. He asked himself. Or made Mary ask for him. And don't call me Log in front of the others.'

They found David in the Mill Reef bar, at a table lined at intervals with champagne bottles and surrounded by young men Adam did not know. A halo of good cheer encircled David's head and his glasses sparkled in the sunlight. He rose heavily as they approached. He wore a morning-coat piped with black silk, a flowered waistcoat and Pop trousers. He did not look fake.

'Laura,' he bellowed and then more softly, 'Laura,

Adam, have some foul champagne. You know Oliver Thwaite and Poppy. The others must introduce themselves.'

David giggled. The young men leaned forward or stood up to give their names to Laura but Adam was looking at Poppy, the same who had been removed so spectacularly from David's last party. She had pretty Chinese eyes, a big bosom and short, lubricious legs; but her hair was damp and she shivered.

'Hello, Poppy.' Adam sat down beside her.

'Adam, I've heard so much about you from Oliver.' She leaned her heavy bosom against his arm. 'I don't mind not coming with you to Kent,' she breathed softly into his ear. Adam noticed sweat on her upper lip.

'I think Laura has a problem with room.'

'I don't mind if you look after Ollie for me.' She scratched her arms vigorously and picked up a glass. 'Ollie darling, will you get me another g-and-t?'

'I've lost a fortune, Adam,' David shouted down the table happily.

'Paquet obstructed Piggott,' said Oliver, ignoring Poppy. 'I was standing with Billy von Schlesien and he . . .'

'Watch it, mate. Dad's the steward.' Mary had appeared with Laura's father. 'Well, aren't we having fun at the expense of the working-man? It won't be long now, you know.' There was a commotion of young men and chairs.

'Let's find Toby.' Laura got up.

'Yes, Toby,' said Mary sadly. 'Divide and rule. Divide and rule. That's the English way.' They all got up except Poppy.

They found Toby in the main car park, pacing up and down by David's big car, his hands clasped behind his back. The boy in the safari suit was sharing a flask of something with Henry, David's chauffeur-cum-butler.

'Not the most profitable day's racing, quite frankly,' Toby said. 'But for a stable tip this bloke had . . .'

David hurried them to the cars before the newcomer could be introduced.

★

53

'I like that.' Toby was already seated before a hillock of fried food as the others straggled into breakfast. 'I accept an invitation from Henry to try and make up my losses at dominoes in the pub. Quite reasonable or not? And what do I find? That Oliver and Mary have been distributing Chinese heroin to all and sundry.'

'Mary!' said David

'The police,' Mrs Eggins said, pounding round the table with the tea. 'The only way to save their lives, I say.'

'I particularly resent Adam's conduct . . .'

'Oh come on, Toby. Anyway, I'm sure Oliver will offer you some.'

'I haven't got any,' Oliver said, twisting in his seat and blinking, 'any more.'

'Mary! I'm speechless.'

'I agree,' said Mary. 'In fairness, Oliver dear, if you have drugs, you should share them with all your friends rather than pick and choose.'

David looked at Adam, who turned away, and then at Laura at the head of the table but she sat still and silent, sipping Mrs Eggins' tea.

After breakfast, Laura and her father left, arm in arm, for church. Toby began devising a whisky cocktail for the others in the tatty drawing room. David wandered, picking out books from the shelves and replacing them.

'I must leave after lunch. I have some business in London,' he said.

'Poor David,' said Mary.

'I mean would you like a lift? Or anybody?'

'Yes, please,' Oliver said. 'I've got to see someone too.'

'What a good idea,' said Toby, straightening from his mess at the flooded drinks table. 'Might I come too?'

David seemed to regret his haste; but no sooner were Laura and Sir Donald sighted by the wicket from the church and Caruso and Patti, the spaniels, barking feebly at the front door, than Toby was chivvying Oliver towards the Bentley and Henry had his cap on. David's apologies were interminable. Oliver looked back once, blinking furiously, at the women waving goodbye on the steps and then was drawn away in a keening of spaniels, his little head weaving between those of the two men beside him, one very much richer than he, and one much stronger.

'Oh dear, poor Oddjob,' said Mary, putting her arms roughly round Adam's neck as he stood a step below her. 'He deserves it, of course, but they might kill him.'

During lunch, it began to rain in sheets for the first time since the Sunday at Helle. There was little conversation. The darkness outside seemed to confirm Sir Donald's habitual gloom and he stared for long periods at Mrs Eggins' fishcakes, or suddenly patted Mary's hand on his left, or looked down the table past Adam shovelling his boiled rice to Caruso, at his daughter, trembling at the head of the table. As Mrs Eggins brought in the spotted dick, Sir Donald jumped up and walked out and, a little later, Adam thought he heard singing.

'Ah Adam,' Sir Donald said suddenly from the door. 'I wonder if you would help me for a moment. I need your advice on my books.'

'Of course,' said Adam reluctantly, scratching his arms.

Outside in the hall, Adam *could* hear singing. As he followed Sir Donald down the dark passage, it separated itself into a female voice and a great deal of hiss.

The room they entered was chaos. Books and magazines lay in unstable piles on the shelves or formed a palisade round a torn horsehair sofa. A glass of whisky stood at the sofa's head beside an old mono gramophone, the source of the singing now recognisable as of *Sonnambula*.

'You must be dying for a drink.' Sir Donald gestured at a table of bottles against his cluttered desk. He stepped towards the table, then stopped, and made his way back with a pile of books which he handed Adam.

'Is that Callas?' Adam looked for a place to take his pile of books.

Sir Donald stopped with his hand on the machine and looked at Adam vaguely. 'Ah, you know it, of course. Milan. I was there. Jocelyn Ambrose took me up from Rapallo.'

'Oh, I didn't know you were friends, Laura didn't . . .'

Sir Donald's eye had now passed over Adam's head. Islanded among the books, Adam cast a glance round at a large picture above the desk, a portrait of a woman in a black velvet dress, petting a greyhound. She might have been Laura, but that her eyes had a spark and were black not blue.

'Ah yes, my wife. Lady Penrose. Quite a good likeness. She was a singer, too.' He bent his head ot one side and closed an eye as if to shut out the hiss from the gramophone. He raised his arm as the finale scurried to an end. 'It wasn't her fault,' he said. 'She was sleepwalking, you know.' He threaded his way back towards the drinks table. 'I'm afraid there's only whisky or water.'

Adam moved a framed photograph to make room for his pile of books. The photograph was of Johnny, his shirt open, the sun in his eyes. Behind him was a churning ferris wheel.

'Johnny takes after me. My father was red too. My darling, of course, takes after her mother.'

'I took the photograph,' In fact, Said had taken it, having sulked till Johnny agreed.

'You're another great Beirutian, aren't you? I haven't been back for years. I knew old Père Gemayel. He's rather a back number now, isn't he? Son's a bit of a thug, I heard.'

'Bachir is, but they say he's getting a bit more polish.' Adam wondered if Sir Donald wanted to make a point. Down the passage, Laura called out time to leave.

Sir Donald was looking at the floor. 'You'll be going back, I take it.'

'No. I don't think so for the moment.' Adam turned to go.

'Is it because of the American? He said.' Sir Donald recoiled at his boldness.

'I'm not sure I follow. I'm not going back because I'm trying to finish my book on the Palestinians.' Sir Donald was now looking out into the soft drizzle. 'I'm not going back, Sir Donald, because the Israelis are going to invade Lebanon.'

'Of course. Is that what they were saying in Beirut?'

'Yes. I'm sorry, Sarabi was saying that. I mean it depends on opportunity and provocation and nobody knows how far they will want to go.' Laura called out more sharply. 'They're terrific opportunists.'

'Of course. Butterworth thinks they will go as far as the city. You know Butterworth, don't you?'

'Isn't he at the Foreign Office?'

'No.' Sir Donald turned round. 'By size, language or topic? Subject, language, size? I can't decide.' But Laura was standing in the door.

They set off through the drizzle, Sir Donald waving them farewell for ever from the steps. Laura lay down immediately in the back seat.

'Not the soul of gaiety, old Donald,' Mary said at length.

Adam cast a glance into the back seat but Laura was asleep. 'I think he's worried about Johnny. Can't see why. Seems to want me to go and look after him.'

'Blind leading blind. Anyway, the old boy needs a chick, that's what. I'd do it for him, if he wanted, but he's not very forward and one can't make all the running.' She moved her legs together under the steering-wheel.

'Don't do that, Mary. You don't mean it.'

'He never got over her.'

'Yes, what happened to her? Laura is so blasted secretive.'

'She went to Africa. That place where they grow coffee and drink all day and all the blokes are called Jack.'

'Kenya? The White Highlands? Is that still going?'

'Yes, Kenya. She was a singer. Not a very good one, Dad says, but beautiful. Everyone was madly in love with her and she chose him. Only Johnny is his, of course.'

'For God's sake, Mary.' Adam glanced again at the curled-up figure in the back.

'I think she came to a bad end.'

'That sort of tart always does.'

'I shan't,' said Mary.

At Clements Street, they could not find Oliver. Henry was leafing through Mary's picture catalogues. Toby paced the floor. On the sofa, a young man in a safari suit was stretched out, asleep. The room stank of amyl nitrate.

'How often have I told you not to take that thing in here.' Mary stamped her foot. 'What's wrong with the garage? Anyway, what have you done with Oddjob?'

'Ah,' said Toby.

Henry looked up from his book. 'Mr Thwaite became angry because Toby pulled out some of his hair.'

'Toby?'

'Well, we had a few people round. Henry borrowed some drink from Hans Place. Smoked a bit of smack. Quite a reasonable evening.' He averted his eyes from the young man on the sofa, who was snoring lightly. 'Oddjob tried to ban me on some trumped-up charge and in my own, or rather your, house. You know what he's like, cutting it up upstairs with everybody round him with their tongues hanging out, while he lays down the law about his grand friends. I tried to remonstrate with him. Rather roughly, I'm afraid.' Toby slapped his thigh.

Mary nodded gravely. She passed over to the sofa.

'Ah. That's Smith. He's a bookie at Catford and Henry thought he might be useful but, unfortunately, he passed out in the car on the way from David's.'

'You can't stay here,' Mary said, shaking the young man gently. He did not stir. Mary turned on the chauffeur accusingly. 'Can't you take him back?'

'I'm not a taxi, Miss Mark, Miss Penrose. More like a bus.' He replaced his book carefully in the shelves. The young man rose smartly to his feet and stared at them in turn.

'Quite reasonable,' he said.

'Toby could make him up a bed down here,' said Laura dubiously. Mary reached into her bag and handed Adam a £10 note. 'Be an angel, Adam, and show Mr Smith the way to the taxi rank.'

Adam had to propel him to Sloane Street for, though he walked quite straight, he became overcome with thought at each street corner. Once in the taxi, he half-woke and looked closely at Adam holding the door.

'There is no monopoly of violence, you know,' he said.

Adam intrigued against Oliver. Mary took no notice. Poppy was a better bet, for Mary thought her a mere screw-tart and possibly half-witted and even Laura could not fail to notice her turning her pretty Chinese eyes on Toby or laying a light hand on his wrist. But one hot afternoon, as Adam struggled with his paper Palestinians and scratched his arms, Poppy arrived from her shopping and they made love with enthusiasm and not a little violence. Adam kept silent after that. Oliver remained, presiding over his mirror and his large-denomination banknotes, and conducting his queer monologues of business and royalty. His head was marked by small stitches where a surgeon had woven in new hair.

The weekends were Mary's domain. Adam was transported through the scorched countryside to large houses: in the Cotswolds, where they sat in hot gardens and talked Capital Transfer; or Shropshire, where they visited neighbours; or Scotland, where they sat on club fenders and talked ghosts; or Hampshire, where Adam struck too late; or Surrey, where they admired Miss Jekyll; or poor Sir Donald's Kent.

They lost money at Goodwood. At Deauville, Adam put his arms round Riverrun's perfect neck under the chestnuts, though he had won a tenth of what he had gambled; but Laura and Adam bathed in the sea and Mary stayed up all night at blackjack in a set of painted widows and won the cost of the aircraft and the hotel and Toby's right to lie snoring in the casino bar.

The Palestinians! They went to dances, in pink marquees smelling of paraffin or ballrooms still damp with disuse while shy mamas looked on at the little girls and the ageing young men, not counting the cost but a little surprised that the Luca Giordano had to go with the dance floor so empty and the young girls so sour. Yet these too seemed to end the same way, in a locked library or maid's bedroom, with Oliver, smuggled in like a foundling, holding his mirror or glassed picture.

Palestinians! One morning, as Mary and Adam drove from one dance to the other, possibly better – the Guercino, perhaps – he proposed going to his sister's in Wiltshire to complete Ambrose's paper. Mary thought this a good idea and suggested he spend the night of the Bath conference at Helle.

CHAPTER FIVE

Lydia was Adam's favourite sister.

She was two years older and their childhood closeness, though interrupted by Adam's boarding schools and Lydia's occasional alliances with Lavinia, seemed to have been ever more intimate as their memories of Brightwell dimmed. It was a submerged rock on which they could stand when tide or current brought them together.

As much the younger of the two girls, Lydia had had no opportunity at Brightwell to assume their dead mother's mantle which Lavinia had seized and belted on with the help of uncles and solicitors and, later, a more than respectable husband. Faced with a *coup*, Lydia supported or undermined her elder's position according to how she conceived her own interests until marriage to the doctor, who loathed his own family and hence all families, enforced a truce.

Yet she had hardly settled in Wiltshire before she was outdoing Lavinia in sternness and organisation and the production and disciplined upbringing of children.

Lydia made up in energy what she lacked in experience. She had met the aspiring doctor at university in London but it was three more years and an exhaustive study of natural history in South Kensington before she came round to the view – or learned, as she put it – that it is better to marry a good man who is not irritating than some more ambitious figure from the world of learning or the City. For Harold, immediately at their marriage and with evident relief, bought a small stone house near Malmesbury and set himself up with country illnesses.

At first, Lydia had much to occupy her: in producing her three children and supervising extensions to the house to accommodate them; in listing and publishing the species grown or found in the Malmesbury area; and in achieving a comparable intimacy with all about her, the rich who needed her advice on how to keep their gardens but release their gardeners – 'groundcover' was Lydia's watchword – the poor through her activity in church business and good causes.

Soon even this varied life proved too little to fill the day. Lydia returned to the affairs of the Murray family in its larger sense. Amid the heaped post at Clements Street, Adam would often come on circulars typed on onion-skin paper, his initials underlined in red at the top, on any matter from the ownership of a piece of furniture to some intricate project for a Christmas reunion.

The latest had been occasioned by a loose remark from Adam about the pendant Cupid and Psyche at Helle and attached an opinion from a local authority that, indeed, the Brightwell Sir Joshua was the original and the Helle picture a late and undistinguished copy.

George Murray was not consulted on this, or indeed any other, matter for the girls thought him at best erratic and at worst embittered, although this was innovation; for Adam did not remember his mother utter any such opinion unless her refusal to alter the arrangement of the house and the pictures that he had undertaken with such care amounted to an opinion.

The clue was here, Adam had thought as he had read the cylostyled judgment. The attribution to Reynolds of a picture now in Pittsburg was necessary, for was it not part of a canonical view of their lost Brightwell and a nod to their delicious sense of loss?

Lavinia allowed the circular to pass, though not, of course, unacknowledged for she had the writing-desk from Brightwell and leisure to write. Her letter to Adam began with the dim recollection, which hardened overleaf into certainty, of a day in the drawing room when their mother, dusting, had said the Sir Joshua should pass to Adam. It was therefore a grave mistake to have sold it as she had said at the time but nobody had listened even when she had proposed it hang, for a transitional period, in her own household.

In these little skirmishes, Adam was impartial or, rather,

he supported the sister to whom he happened to be talking. They seemed to recognise his support as fickle but also to value it, for he was the son, and heir though to nothing, and alone enjoyed correct relations with George Murray, who was their father. Lydia was pleased to receive him for a two-week stay.

She liked activity around her and insisted that Adam spread his typewriter, notes and cuttings along the table in the dining room she had reclaimed from the garden. She would sit with him, rocking the infant of the three children in a large pram that seemed more suited to Kensington Gardens than Wiltshire and knitting slowly.

She did not talk to him, unless he showed clear signs of restlessness, and he made progress though he felt sick and giddy. Lydia prescribed country air and Adam would spring up to join her whenever she proposed a walk to get London out of him.

Adam enjoyed these excursions though he felt for Abigail and Charlotte as they walked the hot country roads in their velvet collars. Lydia could answer every question about what grew or buzzed or darted and Adam, who had seen only dying elms, saw each was dying in its own way. He did not mind that he was not allowed to smoke on the walks, for Lydia was worried about drought and fire.

She was also a greedy woman and although Harold was not, as Toby had spotted, 'much of a drinker', Lydia made sure Adam did not starve or thirst. The first evening, when Adam thought he must burst with restlessness and the empty ache in his chest, he drank the entire half-bottle of Isle of Wight wine which Harold had put out to celebrate his arrival. The next day, the doctor returned from Malmesbury with two cases of claret.

As one blue day followed another, the residue of the drug left Adam. He stopped scratching. He felt dizzy only in coming in from the garden, where Lydia would be deadheading in disintegrating boots, and entering the cool, dark dining room where his papers awaited him. He still slept badly but when he quietly asked the doctor for a sleeping draught, Lydia intervened and set Adam to the most menial tasks, hoeing or tending the tulip sapling from

Brightwell or sawing branches off the *sorbus* till his back ached and he lay under the sprinkler on the lawn. That night he slept.

The lecture assumed shape and authority. Adam had to try out the conclusions on Lydia and the doctor, for they read *The Times* with care each morning and evening respectively, and retained the country person's interest in foreign affairs.

'But it was the terrorists who caused Lebanon to disintegrate,' she said late one afternoon as she knitted away, unmindful of the dropped stiches that would appear as holes in the front of Abigail's next good jumper. Lydia was experimenting with purl stitch.

'Well,' said Adam, his mind going blank as it always did when he was discussing the question rather than addressing his typewriter. 'You know the Palestinians are homeless, squatters, as it were. Squatters never look after a place they occupy.'

'How's Toby?' She looked up from her knitting and then smiled in embarrassment at the connection of thought.

'All right.' Toby's visit, in company with Mary on their return one Sunday from Helle, had been a failure. Lydia had found suspicious butt-ends in the compost.

She looked up sharply. The two little girls had entered and were sitting silently on the chairs against the wall, swinging their legs.

'Go and play, you two.'

'We've run out of things to play,' said Abigail boldly.

'Abigail! Don't be so childish. What about the copulating sedges?'

'They've stopped.'

'Well, there's lots to do in the garden. You might find slugs where Uncle Adam has been sprinkling.'

The two girls got up reluctantly and ran into the garden. Lydia returned to her knitting. 'Harold doesn't have much time for people who don't work,' she said. The doctor was outside, engaged in some husbandly task to do with wood.

'Come on. He's working in Harrods' food halls. He gets things.' Adam stopped just in time. 'At specially reduced rates.'

'That's what I mean. He's got a degree of sorts, hasn't he?' Lydia, alone of Adam's circle but Johnny, had taken a first.

Adam wanted to say that there was something on Toby which had nothing to do with work or duty or success, a quality hard to name but which sometimes made Adam smile when he thought of him, a quality more Irish than Scots: that he could set a room of people to animated conversation, could browbeat the most jaded or ill-assorted group to one more expedition, could give glamour to the most routine activity; that he had ever been the pointsman in their lives, presiding over couplings and smashes without malice or intention. Adam could not say all this here, with Lydia struggling to pick up a stitch and the dim sound of sawing from an outhouse and the children on their knees through the French window, trustingly searching the brown, damp lawn for slugs. All this activity, he thought; all this activity. Even the child in the pram seemed busy in some way, examining the world beneath the pram-hood with an intensity that could not fail to be of use later in life. 'Oh, Lyd, for God's sake, we can't all be moving mountains in Miss Jekyll boots.'

'I know, I know. They are a bit obvious, aren't they?' She smiled in confusion. 'But you know what people are like in the country. They expect one to look the part; I suppose, so that they don't have to look any further. I, great naturalist type; you, great Arabist type. Which reminds me. What are you going to do after the conference, after Bath?' The clicking of needles had stopped.

'I don't know, Lyd. I was thinking of going back to Beirut. I mean, after the book. Johnny is there.'

'Good mind, Johnny,' she said quickly. 'But Harold thinks he's wasting it a bit. I'm surprised he was turned down by the Foreign Office with his degree and his father.' The needles had started up again.

'I don't know. Beirut is so depressing now.'

'Do the *Spectator* have a correspondent there? We don't get the *DT* here, you see, though Lavinia kindly sent your articles. Mrs Davies says it isn't worth her while getting it in on account of there not being demand.' Lydia looked at Adam. 'Poor fellow, you look tired. It's the air here. Still, I'm glad the eczema has cleared up. I'll make some tea.'

The airport was open, he thought. If he came in by air, he would never need to make the crossing. He could stay at the Admiral and the *DT* could pay Boutros directly. He would never need to cross over to the eastern, the Kataib side. How he hated the crossings, not knowing from one day to the next which was open: down along the wide, straight road past Galerie Semaan between fields of maize growing man-high, unharvested, or under the jacarandas beside the Museum, or through the ruins of the port between crumbling red buildings like sandcastles the sea has been at and freighters lying belly-up like dead mackerel; and that time, when the Kataib had finally let him leave in the twilight and he had insisted they make the crossing, how Said had seemed to squash into a ball behind the wheel as they bucked and screeched through the port-sheds, down the barricades of old containers, and there it was, a car, a Citroën and the driver crouched down on the sea side weeping in frustration and fear, and he had thought: Don't stop, Said, don't stop, he'll get us in the face, but Said slowed down and the driver jumped back in and they rammed the car all the way to the Phoenicia till the poor man's boot came loose in the battering. Once in safety, the man forgot the sniper and had tried to make Adam pay for the repairs.

Said would be there, with the red Chevrolet that the Syrian checkpoints recognised and waved through, and Johnny and Hussein Sarabi with his gentle voice. Adam pushed the subject from him. For might not the Israelis come all the way to Beirut, as Sir Donald thought, or link up with the Kataib and then what would happen? Adam was back where he did not want to be, with his lecture.

Against his mild protest, Lydia had taken each sheet as it was completed, typed it onto a banda skin – making small corrections of expression and syntax as she went – and had the whole run off on the press used for the parish magazine. 'That way,' she explained, 'they can all follow what you are saying.' The fifty faint, onion-skin copies sat in neat piles on the dining-room table, awaiting only the conclusion; but here Adam had difficulties.

The argument seemed to make sense: Arafat must renounce war before it was renounced for him; but did he dare and could he survive? 'Progress on our side,' Sarabi used to say as they sat in the Research Institute, 'will come only from a military setback. The Palestine Revolution has ossified.' But did Israel want peace? Or the Kataib? Bachir's men wanted revenge. And Syria? Syria would kill anybody who conspired to leave it facing Israel alone. Adam wanted to tone down the early sections of the paper but had been pre-empted by Lydia's efficiency. She had also hinted, no more, that a visit to church that Sunday might not be amiss given the cost of banda and paper, not to speak of the time taken on a machine dedicated to God's work.

Adam had already seen the Morris window although the church was otherwise, in Lydia's judgement, quite lacking in interest. For devotional purposes, he had not entered a church since Lydia's wedding. Seated now beside her, in a favourable pew and she hatted, he felt sensations of Brightwell: a slight, damp chill, the smell of dust and wax and prayer books, the rough feel of the cold heating-pipe under their seat.

Lydia prayed on her knees, at length and without ostentation. Adam opened his prayer book and saw again marvellous sentences. He turned to the Commination, but Lydia had now risen and was commenting on the few other members of the congregation scattered in some system of their own along the nave and on who had and who had not rallied to the successful struggle she had led against the New Service.

'Harold goes to evensong and the girls to Sunday School. That way we spread ourselves out a bit. There are so few young people now.'

It had not occurred to Adam to consider her young in the sense that he, Adam, was or Mary or Laura. The Morris window caught the sun and colour streaked the wrought-iron screen before the choir. It was a Resurrection. Christ, half-out of the tomb, seemed one of Lydia's brilliant emerging butterflies; the tomb-lid was cracked; soldiers dozed among lilies. How had all this come about?

Why, why, why, if the universe is adequately explained without God, why propose him? Or rather, since religion is no better at explaining the universe than no religion, why submit to it? Adam tried to concentrate on the sermon, which was about soldiers sleeping (among the lilies, at the Museum), but his thoughts drifted their agnostic way. The choir sang an anthem, overcome by a flat mezzo-soprano with a strong Wiltshire accent. This was Mrs Davies, newsagent and tobacconist. Lydia took the collection and her hat shook with her suppressed laughter when she came to Adam. After the service, he waited for her in the porch.

'A most instructive paper, Adam, if I might so address you.' The vicar had a neat soldier's figure and white hair. Adam was appalled by his presumption. 'I was stationed in Palestine during the war, as you heard in my short address, and was of the hope that Jew, Muslim and Christian of every denomination could live there in harmony with Jerusalem truly the capital of the world. But it was not to be.' He smiled sadly and greeted a group of ladies passing through the porch. 'Mrs Warburton tells me you will be returning to that tormented region.'

'Well, that is not yet certain.' Adam crossly joined Lydia under the yew-tree.

'£6 in the collection and I put in five,' she said laughing as they walked back up the high street. 'I must say, Adam, you could have done better. Mean lot, all of you.'

'Look, Lydia, do you believe all that nonsense?'

'Which? The Angel of the Eighth Army? Not particularly. We have it once or twice a year.'

'No, I mean God, the intercession of Christ, birth, crucifixion, death and resurrection, life after death, you know.'

'At some times more than others,' she replied carefully from under her dreadful hat. 'I like the language and Harold likes me to go and otherwise there would be nobody in church and they might as well let it fall down. Then there's faith, but Adam, that's not so much the leap into the abyss as Kierkegaard was always saying; it's more like a slide down the side, hanging onto things as you go.' She looked pleased with her simile.

'But there's no evidence.'

'Yes, there jolly well is. Once you have a belief of sorts then all the bits and pieces are evidence. Did I ever tell you how some lepidoptera lay eggs, under water, taking a bubble of air down with them, under their wings? Anyway, your mother liked us to go.'

'Oh, do stop it.'

She put her arm through his. 'What a revolting black-head! Doesn't Mary do them for you?'

Harold drove him to Bath that evening. Adam made a show of declining but the bus took four hours and Adam knew that he had expected to be driven.

'Keep your head down,' said Lydia, kissing him good-bye. 'If I don't see you before you go.'

The day was out of breath. The birds in the dead trees sounded parched in their calls and the brooks were dry or a trickle. Smoke from burning stubble came in through the open window.

Adam felt nervous as he sat with Harold in the Volvo. It was not that they did not talk, for the doctor kept up a stream of polite questions, but Adam sensed he was not remotely interested in the replies. He was missing evensong where Lydia liked him to take the collection.

'I liked Toby, you know,' he said suddenly. 'I know Lydia thinks he should have a proper job but isn't that up to him? Anyway, there isn't really enough work to go round, is there, any more? In Germany, even, I read; and often I have nothing to do at the surgery.'

Adam remembered, when they brought Lukomski up to the Frères, there were playing cards on the table, in three untidy piles, where the surgeons had broken off their game.

'Aren't you tempted by the hurly-burly of London?'

'No. Lydia wanted to live in the country for her insects and plants and I agreed with her. I think place is the most important thing, belonging to a place, if you see what I mean.' He paused, wondering perhaps if he had said more than he meant, but he seemed unable to leave the subject. 'Lydia says you can tell the age of a hedgerow by the

68

number of tree species in it. Each one a hundred years. The one in the field behind the house has ash, oak and that lime thing, Lydia knows its name. That means three hundred years.

'I wonder if the tulip tree will grow as large as the one at Brightwell. Lydia says the Brightwell one is the biggest in England, bigger even than the one at Petworth.' He stopped, embarrassed and went back to his questions. 'Were you sad to leave Brightwell?'

Adam thought for a moment. 'No, not really. It was getting rather ratty and it was nice being a guest all the time. I am a guest-rather than a host-type. I suppose I could live all my life in hotels.'

'Oh, could you?' Harold looked at him in surprise and then turned quickly back to the road. 'I can't spend a night away from home. Hate it. Hate it. Lydia likes to go to Scotland every year, but with the small child, we shan't be going this year. I can't say I'm too sorry.'

Adam thought of the Admiral, where he could have his old room and the fridge was stocked every day.

CHAPTER SIX

'A formidable piece of work.'

Butterworth was standing in a group beside the common-room bar, dressed in a thick white jumper and holding a cup of coffee. He looked more biscuity than ever. Behind him, three Palestinian students in coats and ties and carrying mugs of beer were playing darts and talking English. The room was dirty and smelled of old cigarette ash.

'Ah Murray,' Butterworth said as Adam joined the group by the bar. 'You'll have to look to your laurels. We have just heard a fine paper from Miss Khalidi on the role of the old Jerusalem families in the PLO power structure. A most helpful and timely contribution.' A dark-skinned girl in tweed and lambswool simpered in embarrassment.

Adam had missed the first session of the conference, still struggling with his conclusion and the manuscript alteration to all fifty copies. These had now been distributed and Adam eagerly awaited an informed judgement. Butterworth detached himself from the group and put his arm on Adam's shoulder.

'Quite a good effort, I felt,' he said quietly. 'I thought you spread the Arafat interview rather thin, although it contained good information. As for Sarabi, and indeed the entire Research Institute circle, I wonder; I sometimes felt that Sarabi entertained an unhealthy interest in Israel and its institutions. You give the misleading impression that Sarabi's interest in a negotiated settlement is capable of a majority; nor did you fully consider Syrian opposition, let alone the attitude of Israel. I would have liked a greater use of Arabic written sources, *al-filistin al-thawra*, and some of the smaller papers. Otherwise, and in the purely military sector, sound.'

'Thank you,' said Adam in some confusion. 'Who is here?'

'For some reason, Ambrose is not coming until tomorrow. I'm afraid Prince Hassan will not be coming after all.' Butterworth raised his voice so that the rest of the group drifted back to him. 'The Minister of Court telephoned me from Amman last night. Arafat sent a telegram, for all the good,' he added under his breath, 'it will do him.'

'So you think the balloon is going up,' Adam said and then added lamely, 'too.'

'Without doubt.' Butterworth turned on him in feigned surprise. Miss Khalidi smiled knowingly. 'It has long been clear that the peace treaty with Egypt frees Israeli resources for large-scale military action against the Palestinians in Lebanon. The signs, as you know, are that the Americans are preparing a peace initiative which Israel must move to forestall. That would suggest this summer raher than next and is why your discussion of the PLO's military options must be a central contribution to this conference.'

Adam trembled slightly as Butterworth continued his analysis, but now to Miss Khalidi, whom he gallantly took into lunch, one hand resting on her buttock.

'You a don too?' Adam's neighbour had a boyish look and wore, of all things, a safari suit.

'No, no. A sort of writer. Adam Murray. Haven't we met before?'

'Might have done. William Smith. Don't usually read the *DT* but I quite enjoyed your thing on the Phalangists last year. We should be back there, instead of listening to all this jaw.'

'I don't really want to go back.' Adam found Smith's open face and soldierly manner encouraged confidences. 'Butterworth thinks the invasion is imminent.'

Smith looked down at his ravioli. 'You know, I've done fourteen wars for the paper; small wars; rabble. Was a soldier. Father was a bookie. Left school at fifteen. What were you? Eton and King's?'

'No.'

'All rabble. I don't need the Palestinians. I want to do one more with a proper army for the first time in my life. If my bottle holds up, that is.'

'What about the Israelis? Best army in the world, they say.'

'Second best.' Smith pushed his plate away. Adam thought he must be a little drunk.

'All right then, the Kataib. Bachir has polished them up a bit.'

'They're still scum. Anyway, I can't speak French.' Smith closed one eye and looked up at Adam. 'So what do you say in your lecture or whatever it is.'

'The Palestinians will come second.'

'Deserve to. Destroyed every place they've been in without advancing their cause an inch. An inch. Look at Jordan. Look at Beirut. Rabble.'

'Sad, though, don't you think?'

'You're all the same, you public schoolboys. You only like lost causes. The only one of them worth anything was Sarabi. I was with him when he recaptured the Holiday Inn and he handed it back to the Lebs and do you know what they did? They looted the shopping arcade! Rabble. Sarabi was at least a soldier. Camberley.'

'Did you see him after he went to the Research Institute?' Adam was stung by Butterworth's denigration of his best source.

'I heard something odd about him. What was it? My memory is going. Drink.'

They sat through the afternoon together, or rather Adam sat, in a welter of nerves, while Smith slumped with his eyes half-closed. They heard an impenetrable Dane on conditions in Sabra Camp; Miss Khalidi moderated a discussion on the emancipation of Palestinian women; and a West Coast professor revealed the results of a computer analysis of the decisions of the Palestine National Council and offered the tentative, and quite unremarkable, conclusion that Palestinians found it hard to agree.

The reading of this paper took so long that by the time Adam joined Butterworth on the platform, time was running out. The audience was beginning to fidget; a new notion, tea, was taking shape above them; Smith was now clearly fast asleep and this was, well, unnecessary.

Butterworth summarised Adam's paper in two crisp sentences and supported the contention that armed struggle, though futile, could not be renounced without a radical change in the PLO's nature. Discussion was thrown open to the floor and immediately got out of hand.

'What is your homeland?' asked one of the dart Palestinians in an accent that Smith, had he been awake, would have placed as King's.

'Scotland,' Adam replied with some hesitation.

'How would you think,' the boy went on, 'if your Scotland were occupied by the . . . by the . . .' He seemed at a loss to find an occupier. 'By the Welsh. Would you not fight to regain your home?'

Adam thought of the damp braes of Argyll colonised by husbanding Welshmen; but a Lebanese had already jumped up and was condemning the Palestinian armed presence in his country while a graduate student in a skull-cap proposed that the Palestinians already had a homeland in Jordan. This brought an angry response from a group of Jordanian diplomats, deputizing for their absent Crown Prince, and Butterworth had some difficulty bringing order to this free-for-all. Adam leaned back, elated that it was all over, conjured £250 and allowed the debate to ebb and flow before him.

The elation continued through tea for Adam found himself surrounded by people asking questions they had been too shy or discreet to ask in the open session. He found himself slipping into Butterworth language. With Miss Khalidi, he discussed the role of women in the armed struggle and they agreed that it was a topic that merited further and systematic consideration. He noticed for the first time that she was quite pretty and had expensive shoes. Only Smith, sitting quietly by the dartboard in the safari suit that seemed too big for him, mocked Adam's self-importance.

'Talk. All talk,' he said as Adam joined him. 'Let's go and have a drink in a pub. I can't take much more of this.'

73

'I can't. I have to stay with a friend in Somerset. We'll meet again, won't we?'

'Do you want to go back?' Smith peered up at him through the corner of his eye. 'I'm sure the *DT* will take you back on a superstringer basis. I'll talk to them, if that would help.

'Come on. Give the old Admiral one more whirl and we'll get Boutros to tape up the windows this time.'

'Let's see how the situation develops.'

Adam was packing in his room when the door opened, revealing Butterworth. He looked impatient. 'Off, already. I had hoped you and Leila Khalidi would lead the discussion on South Lebanon. You, after all, have visited Beaufort Castle.'

'I'm terribly sorry.' Adam felt acutely the piles of dirty washing in his suitcase but did not think he could close the lid without drawing attention. 'I'm expected in Somerset tonight.'

'Delightful young woman with a first-rate brain,' Butterworth said. 'She was most enthusiastic about your paper.' He swept the room briskly with his eyes. 'So what next?'

'Back to London. Try and get on with the book.' Adam found Butterworth's vast presence in the room unsuitable, almost suggestive.

'I imagine I'll be collecting the more interesting papers into a volume and do a short introduction myself. Clearly, yours would be a strong candidate given that the focus will be on the military side over the next few months. This would sharply improve your chances of finding an academic publisher for your own book.'

'Aren't events moving a bit fast for all these books?' Adam said truculently.

'Yes. Let me be frank with you, Murray. Sir Donald would like young Penrose to leave Beirut as soon as possible and before the situation deteriorates further. I am sure you could persuade him to leave. You'll be at the Admiral, I would imagine.' He turned to leave.

'Johnny Penrose is a superb Arabic speaker,' Adam said with growing confidence. 'He has excellent contacts,

Lebanese and Palestinian, and is well established at the Research Institute. It's for him, not Sir Donald, to decide.'

Butterworth sat down on a chair impatiently. 'First, General Sharon is a military officer of dash and ambition, and a political imbecile. There is quite a strong possibility that he will go all the way to Beirut and therefore the entire security constellation will alter. Second: the Palestine Research Institute is passing through a period of crisis. Hussein Sarabi has not been re-elected to the PLO Executive Committee and, as far as we can see, is not even handling the Hebrew monitoring. Young Penrose's position is, to a certain extent, affected. Third: young Penrose's written papers were outstanding, among the very best I have seen. However, his performance in the administrative and committee tests was not up to that standard. He was not nor will ever be regular FCO material. I was convinced of this and Sir Donald reluctantly agreed.'

Adam sat down on the bed.

'I do not wish to bully you about the Lukomski affair.'

Adam stared at his shoes. The toes were scuffed and he had no polish. He hoped nobody else was at Helle.

'As you well imagine, the Americans are still livid about his death. They were not at all impressed by the reports from the Kataib and the Lebanese Army Deuxième Bureau. Nor was I for that matter.' He stood up to leave. His sparsely covered head almost touched the ceiling. 'It is not for me to judge you. Automatic fire in a built-up environment can be unsettling. But I understand there is some interest in Jerusalem to follow up the investigation, partly as a present to the Americans and partly, I would have thought, to scotch the impression in Washington that they had a hand in it.'

'That's impossible. He was hit in the back. From Sodeco, from the Western side . . .'

'Well done, Murray. Clearly, they would wish to speak to you since you came through the Museum that day.'

'Not true. I spent the night in Jounieh.'

'I see absolutely no point in squandering information on you. But think for a moment. What would be the most elegant explanation for all concerned? Rather neatly confirmed by Sarabi's current difficulties, I would say.' Butterworth opened the door.

'Wait. I don't understand. Lukomski and Sarabi never met. Lukomski was an East Beirut man.'

'The only connection between the two is you, whether you like it or not. Will you remember me to Mrs Mark, if she is at Helle? I believe she is, although Mark is collecting in Peru. Ambrose may have arrived. Rather a spent force, in my view, but Molly seems to like him. What a trial to her her daughter's friends must be! You have a way of messing things up, Murray, even in Chelsea.' He looked at Adam with contempt and closed the door behind him.

Perhaps, Adam thought, the taxi-driver might have shoe polish. They carried the strangest things in their cars; although not, perhaps, as strange as Said's nickel-plated AK-47 and two hand-grenades.

Mrs Mark was alone. Ambrose was dining in his room and although she had dressed, the servants had been released for the evening. They helped themselves at a small table in the dining-room. The food had been left out in silver dishes over spirit lamps and two decanters of wine stood ready for Adam. Mrs Mark ate only boiled rice and drank water.

The curtains had been drawn and the candles on the little table made little impression on the darkness. Adam could sense rather than see the portraits trembling in their golden frames, Titian's calm Englishmen or Clouet's great brute of a king, looking at them without interest like wild beasts at the edge of a campsite.

'Talk. All talk.' Adam felt he needed to throw his voice before this silent but exacting audience. 'There's going to be the most unholy battle, we all think so, even William, William Smith, but they talk about it as if it were a seminar at a rival university.'

'I know.' Tired, or simply alone, Mrs Mark had lost the bell-like ring to her voice. 'But people are like that. Look at the letters from the front in the Great War.' Her voice would drop, sighing, to the end of the phrase until the breath became too slight to carry it and it cracked like a twig.

'I don't want to go back.' The room with its teeming darkness, the candles and the heavy claret, were turning Adam's misery into heroic acceptance.

'Oh Adam. Will you need to?' She implied duty not menace.

'Do you know Mr Butterworth? He asked that I give you his regards.' Adam smiled to himself but she did remember.

'Oh yes, he shot here once. Wasn't he God at the Foreign Office; yes, when Billy had a job? Well, not really the Foreign Office, the other thing like Jolly in the old days. Knows about those funny miniatures.' She stopped suddenly. 'Is he being tricky?'

'A bit.'

'Oh dear, Adam. It's not about, you know, Clements Street?' She spoke with great difficulty. Adam realised with a start of distress that they had been speaking at cross-purposes, that Mrs Mark, her phrases ending without breath, was not interested in a battle that might or might not take place miles away but in her daughter and her daughter's household.

To have said 'Yes' would have been inaccurate but to have said 'No' would have been to ignore Butterworth's parting remark which had seemed to Adam, as he slumped in the country taxi from Bath to Helle, almost as threatening as the other thing. Then he felt the portraits stir, shift their ancient weight infinitesimally from stockinged foot to stockinged foot, and he regretted his calculation.

'I just don't know.' Adam looked up. 'I'm sorry. I'm not making much sense. I don't think London is doing any of us much good.'

Mrs Mark poured him some coffee and stared out into the darkness. 'Mare's job was never very satisfactory,' she said, 'finding all those wonderful pictures just for somebody else. Do you think she'll get another or wait a bit?'

'What?'

Mrs Mark looked at him carefully. 'Of course, you've been away beavering at your lecture. I did think your sister's article in *Nature* was good. How she has room for all that Greek!'

'Has Mary given up the gallery?' Adam felt desperately foolish but Mrs Mark was too tactful to continue or, perhaps, was loath to volunteer information even to her daughter's intimate friend.

'She's such a funny thing. Still, people must do what they like.'

Adam wanted to make a declaration about himself, that he did love Mary and that – he felt the portraits huge in their gold frames – he would marry her if he could get a bit of money, real money, not evens on Riverrun at Newmarket. At least that would end all this futile activity, not knowing what they were doing till they did it, never knowing what it was for.

Mrs Mark forestalled him. She rose from the table, snuffing all but one of the candles. 'I'm to bed. Never saw the point of staying up. One only worries about the things one hasn't done. But you stay up. You know where the drinks are outside. Take that port with you.' With the remaining candle, she lit Adam all the way to the door. 'Andrew will take you to the 7.50. Breakfast at quarter past. Come and say goodbye before you go. I'm bound to be up.'

Adam slumped down in a sofa in the drawing room. A wood fire was burning. He listened. The house was silent. The house swarmed with silence. Perhaps somewhere in that building the size of a village, someone was awake, Andrew polishing shoes or Mrs Mark still poring over accounts in bed, her spectacles at the end of her nose. Adam could not hear them, could hear nothing unless it was the tick of the clock above the fireplace; and another clock, out in the passage beside the visitor's book, and a third somewhere else and a fourth with a deep and slow movement. Adam heard nothing but clocks, keeping time for the guests.

'Absurd,' said Adam out loud and opened the photograph album. He saw the young shooters on the moor, their faces as flushed as their salmon-pink socks and the young women handing them things and smiling; or Sweet Nothing in the paddock at Longchamp with Mary towering over Piggott as he carried his saddle to the weighing room.

Then Adam did hear something: a step miles away down the dark passage; the nightwatchman, perhaps. He listened and heard the little grate of claw on polished board and the swish of a lady's dress.

'Silly, isn't it?' said Mrs Mark, standing before him. 'Even in a dump as big as this, one still has to put a dog out.' She laughed lightly. 'Much further to go, too.'

She made no attempt to leave and the dog lay down on the carpet. Adam wondered if he should offer her something, her own drink in her own house and at this late hour.

'You can't just blame it on all this,' she said at last, extending her hand a fraction to embrace the room. 'You know she had an awful accident riding out when she was young. We were frantic and, I suppose, we let her do what she liked. And then at the beginning, it was a bit tricky; we were just getting the house in order and Billy was abroad a lot, in Nepal and places like that. And we should have done something about her mouth, you know. But look at Ferd. Who could be fitter than him?' She turned to leave as if she had said too much. The dog lifted itself from the carpet. 'You know, she was never going to just settle down as we all did. And she seemed so happy when she became friends with Toby and you, at the beginning.'

'Do take care, all of you,' she said as she vanished into the dark passage. 'And in the Lebanon, of course, if you go.' Adam heard her steps fade down the long passage but the scratching of the dog's claws on the polished wood continued for a while.

Adam walked out into the passage, to the malachite table covered in bottles. He wanted something, sombre, yet rich, warm in tone but cold in the throat. The malt whiskies at the back were medicinal or peaty, vodka had no taste and gin required additives of a cloying sweetness; port was too round and brandy heady while the champagne, encased in its cylinder of ice, might be fizzy or thin; and opening the bottle would make a noise, or the foil or the wire would scratch on the malachite or he would spill some and disturb the silence of the clocks. 'Absurd,' he said.

'Did you see the Dark Lady?'

Adam turned round slowly. Ambrose stood just on the edge of the circle of light. He wore a quilted dressing-gown and a red silk stock. 'Did you see Mr Butterworth's Dark Lady of Bath?' He giggled and took a tiny step closer. 'I know something Mr Butterworth doesn't know. Your clever friend has disappeared. Quite vanished. It is time for the courage of Regulus. Or Mr Butterworth will get into trouble, won't he? With his Jewish friends, won't he? It wouldn't have happened in my day but it's called something different from my day. There were too many traitors, weren't there? It's called SIS, I believe. Yes, SIS.'

Adam caught his train. He was woken in good time by Mrs Hutchinson, who brought a cup of tea and four tiny slices of buttered bread and opened the curtain on yet another bright day, although perhaps for her it was glare. Adam did not say goodbye to Mrs Mark or Ambrose.

Following Andrew downstairs, Adam did take a last glance at Cupid and Psyche and was stopped short by the differences in the full daylight. He remembered the lady's beckoning hand but there was a look in her eyes he had not noticed: anxiety, perhaps, or need. Delivered at Exeter Station, Adam felt himself cast out into a dingy and hostile world. He bought a first-class ticket.

Clements Street was quiet and Mary's car nowhere to be seen. A mirror had fallen off the wall and stood leaning against the sofa, broken glass still glinting on the floor. All the bottles were empty, even the Campari.

Adam was disappointed. Having not thought much about Mary in the country, or at least not much after he felt better, he had worked himself into a tumult of desire on the train, imagining her just waking in her sunny, dusty room. Adam began to tidy up but soon tired of it and simply cleared a space for his typewriter. He wanted to offer the *DT* an article, prophesying war. He lit a cigarette to think.

The first sentence was the hardest. He listened to the sounds from the mews, the homosexuals on each side tending their window-boxes, the occasional click of heels on the cobbles, the hum of traffic from Sloane Street. He stared up at the ceiling. The rose in the centre had been filled in; the cornice was picked out in red but covered in a line of grey dust. Adam had the odd sensation that the ceiling was bending towards him, as if under a great weight. The first sentence was always the hardest.

Adam listened to the homosexuals chatting to one another as they watered their red geraniums. He could make out, amid the traffic from Sloane Street, engines, horns and car radios. Over it all, he could hear breathing. The walls seemed to be moving in and out with each light breath, as if the house were a diaphragm. Adam walked quietly to the stairs and then up them. On the landing, he hesitated.

Mary's door was just ajar. He could hear the breathing clearly now. It was almost a snore, with the occasional rustle of linen or wool. Adam did not go in. Through the door, he could see a striped shirt hung to air over the back of a chair and a child's grey suit on a hanger from the door knob of the wardrobe.

Adam did not need to go in. He could imagine the white nightgown and the hair spread on the pillow for he had thought of nothing else through the hot countryside from Exeter to Paddington. He did not wish to see the baby she held to her bosom, the strands of hair plastered carefully over the bald crown and the little scabs left by stitches.

Adam walked down into the street and closed the front door quietly behind him.

CHAPTER SEVEN

Mary was smiling her queer half-smile.

'Well, I was smacked out, wasn't I?'

Adam had not known what to expect – shame, at least, or some sort of apology, but not this jauntiness.

'Anyway you went off for two weeks, didn't you?' She was pale and her white skin was of a remarkable translucence he had not noticed before.

He had telephoned Mary and asked her to come to the Ritz, perhaps to assert his authority or, perhaps, to point up in this prettiest of dining-rooms the squalor of her conduct.

She had come docilely enough but Hyde Park had been blocked off, she had said, and the diversion by way of Trafalgar Square had ruined her temper and made Adam wait. The sunshine from Green Park, the painted ceiling or the gilded figures had worked no magic; the food was heavy and the prices well advertised; and Adam could not help thinking of the awful Poppy.

'But with Oddjob, Mary? What are you doing?'

Her grey eyes turned black with anger. 'Oh leave me alone. You're just like all the others. What about your blessed Laura? You didn't bang on to her when he gave her all those mandrax? Like I said, I was all pinned out.'

Adam had not heard the phrase before. 'What? Have you been shooting it up?'

'Doing up? Of course not. Look at my arms.' She held up her arms, bare from her short-sleeved dress and almost transparent in their whiteness, not only to Adam but to the curious butler carving Adam's roast beef. Adam waved at her impatiently.

'See. Not a mark.'

Adam could not look. He sat in silence while he was

served his bloody beef. He felt hot and tired and the claret had gone to his head for Mary was, unusually, drinking nothing and the bottle was his alone. She had, at first, refused to eat but when she saw Adam's impatience, she had hurriedly ordered some boiled rice. Still smiling at Adam, she reached down to her bag and took out a little bottle of pills. She took two hurriedly, grimacing.

'What are those?'

'Some sort of codeine thing. Jolly gave them to me. Says they're good when one's not feeling well.'

'Shut up about Jolly. Can't you see what he's trying to do to you?' Adam summoned the picture of the baby's head but Poppy's spectacular lovemaking intervened. 'Mary, I'm sorry. But don't you think you should give it up altogether as I have. You're losing control of your life. I'm sorry, that's not what I mean. But it seems so nice at the time and then you find the whole world revolves around it, waiting by the telephone all evening like Oddjob. People are getting to hear about it.'

'Who cares what other people think. I knew you shouldn't have stayed at Helle. You just want to be like them, when you're not.' She stopped and smiled again. 'Anyway, we have given it up.'

Adam looked at her in surprise.

'It's just that last night we suffered a relapse. You know how it is and that Toby is such a bad influence. He can never resist a stimulant or a narcotic.' She shrugged her shoulders but went on smiling. 'You shouldn't go away like that.'

Adam felt his nervousness increase. He shifted on his chair and pushed his plate away. He lit a cigarette. He had not planned to say this – nothing he had planned had gone right – but it seemed the right thing to say here, in the Ritz dining-room, with the sunlight pouring in and the painted blue sky above them.

'That's why, Mary, I think . . .' There was still time to stop but the smile so infuriated him. 'Don't you think, I mean, that it wouldn't be a bad idea if we didn't get married?'

Mary opened her mouth and looked at him, startled,

smiling to reveal her teeth. 'Oh Adam, you are nice. But do you mean it?'

'Yes, of course, I do. Otherwise I wouldn't have asked.' Adam was content, that the proposal once made, should carry them along. He leaned back in his chair. He would order a Monte Cristo and a huge glass of Kirschwasser.

'But you're always asking chicks to marry you. Get me a ring and then I'll decide.'

Her composure had returned. She half-closed her mouth. Adam was thinking, but his thoughts led the same miserable conclusion. Since Mary paid for everything at Clements Street, he often had lumps of cash, from articles or Riverrun's unbroken successes, and he would go to Harry's or the Ritz and their very exorbitance made him feel not poor but rich; but a ring, with diamonds and big sapphire, something like that, what did that cost? A ring meant motor cars and a house in the country (he would have to get her out of London), watered-silk sofas and velvet collars; such a good, safe world. Adam looked about him. Monstrous cigars had appeared on every side like weapons in a crowd turning nasty.

'A nice one, too,' said Mary.

He looked at her obstinately. She was softening. 'Poor Adam. I am sorry about the other thing. It makes me sick and he's not coming round to Clements Street again, I can tell you that. Toby will be instructed to push him down the stairs in his inimitable way.'

'That's what I mean, Mary. All this futile, sometimes violent, activity. What's it all for? We think we're civilized. Toby and I went to expensive schools and you can spot a Guido Reni at 200 paces, but we're behaving like barbarians. Laura getting pushed down the stairs and then Oddjob's hair and now this other thing? It's worse than Beirut. We must pull ourselves together.' He stopped. 'That's why marriage might not be such a bad idea.'

'Adam, don't fuss. Let's go home and make it up in bed as they do in books.'

She was sweet on the way home, despite the queue at Hyde Park which was open to only one lane of traffic. As they crawled past a policeman by his motorbike, Adam leaned out and asked what was up.

'I am not empowered to reveal that to members of the public,' the policeman said, leaning into the car and looking Mary cheekily up and down.

'I'm a journalist,' said Adam, making great play of reaching for a Press card in his notecase.

'Well, I will tell you that there has been an incident in Park Lane.'

'A bomb?' asked Mary.

'An incident,' said the officer, standing up so his face was lost.

'IRA?'

'I wouldn't say that.'

'Middle Eastern?'

'Well, if you guessed that, you wouldn't be far wrong.'

'But Adam,' said Mary sweetly as they crawled past the motorbike. 'Why can't they fight their battles in their own countries?'

'Some of them haven't got a country.'

It was not as they do it in books. Mary hurried him upstairs but it seemed to Adam that this hurry was not the hurry of passion but of duty to a mildly disagreeable task and that her pliancy was apology not affection. He lay down beside her. He wondered how they had ever been able to make love.

'So you got fed up with the gallery?' He spoke as neutrally as possible and yet, as he spoke, accusation crept into the sentence.

Mary stirred uneasily. 'Always oversleeping, wasn't I? Missed a sale, didn't I?' Adam hated her new way of speaking. 'Anyway, I wasn't getting anywhere. I know more than those two poofs put together. I'll look round again when we come back from Scotland, won't I?'

Adam wanted to say something but could not. Whatever came to mind seemed weak or bullying when tested against this new Mary. She was kissing him mechanically on the shoulder, her eyes closed. So they stayed in silence until Mary got up for her bath and Adam went downstairs to let

Toby in. With him was Laura, who was carrying the evening newspaper.

Toby, too, looked dejected. In the dining-room, he removed a small parcel from the front of his trousers.

'Another small larceny?'

'Oh, yes. Smoked turkey. I've been rumbled. I knew it would happen.'

'What do you mean?'

'They stopped me on the way out of the tunnel. I had a tin of snails with their shells. Too bulky. I just knew it would happen.'

'Isn't it awful about the shooting in Park Lane?' Laura padded into the dining room with the *Standard*.

'Oh Toby. Poor fellow. Are they going to prosecute?'

'I just don't know. Threatened to. Buggers had my pay packet already there.'

'What does that mean, Adam?'

'What?'

'The shooting in Park Lane?'

'Oh God.' Adam took the paper from her. 'Look, the PLO man has condemned it. We saw the police there. After lunch. It could be agents of an Arab regime.'

'I knew this would happen. Got cocky, didn't I?'

'What will Israel do?'

'£37. Not much for severance pay, is it?'

'They won't prosecute, Toby. They have so many casual staff, nicking things. They won't be bothered.'

'Adam! Pay attention.'

'Laura, sorry. I think the Israelis will retaliate pretty heavily, probably against the Palestinians in Lebanon. The cease-fire doesn't amount to much. The Israelis made it, they can break it.'

'Perhaps I could go to Beirut, if they do start getting heavy. Johnny's there. Is there drink there? Can one drink?'

'To death.'

'Cheer up, To,' said Laura. 'We'll go to David's later and you can get drunk there.'

'Who's been asked?' Adam did not know about the party.

'Mary has. Specifically, only Mary.'

'She can take us all.'

She did, without fuss, but the invitation was for after dinner and she (and Adam) had been included in a dinner-party. Mary was already dressed but seeing Toby and the state he was in, she telephoned the woman and pleaded a sudden visitor. She took them to Harry's where Toby drank a great deal and Adam drank with him. After a while, he found himself repeating the ends of his friends' sentences, which infuriated Toby.

'I don't think I'll come to David's,' Adam said as they emptied into the street. 'I'm feeling rather odd. I think the train journey rather took it out of me.'

'Don't be so feeble, Adam,' Mary said.

'For God's sake,' said Toby, squaring his shoulders. 'Can't you try and behave in a civilized way for once in your life? You don't just bale out in the middle of the evening. We go out to dinner, we go on to a dance. Quite reasonable, or not? You can't pick and choose, you know.' Mary had found a taxi so Adam gave in.

In Hans Place, Adam hesitated before the closed front door, thinking to scent autumn in the breeze; but it was only the tapers flickering each side of the door. Henry the butler opened it, worked down M on his typed list, then added Adam just below Toby.

The rooms were unchanged: the same rich mixture of people, the same sweet champagne. Adam felt he could not support himself. He felt that if he held a glass it would break and cut him or if he leaned against a table, photographs and pot plants and miniatures would tumble and shatter. He turned towards the garden but heard laughter and the sharp scrape of chairs on York stone. He turned instead to the stairs and began to climb.

'Hello, David.' His host was in the bathroom picking champagne bottles out of a bath of ice.

'Hello, Adam. Have a drink.' He passed a bottle which Adam did not think he could support. 'It's not very nice, is it? Still one never learns.'

'One never learns.'

'Are you going back to the Middle East? I heard. Awful about those terrorists in Park Lane.'

'No. Awful. In Park Lane.'

'Morocco, was it?'

David fell silent, picking up a glass from the taps and sipping it ruminatively. Adam still held his bottle but the cork would break something and the wire beneath the foil would cut him.

'I suppose you're looking for Mary?'

'No. Not really. Sweet girl, isn't she?' Adam wandered out and up to the bedroom, where he found his friends among the gigantic nudes.

'Dirty bloke, David,' said Mary from his bed.

Toby was pacing up and down, his shoulders back, doing up his flies.

'Oh, Toby,' said Mary in wonder. 'You're so red in tooth and claw.'

'I'm a bit ashamed of myself, quite frankly,' said Toby and peered out of the window. 'Quiet. I think Poppy is coming.'

She strode into the room, then stood still on her short legs, uncertain suddenly.

'I think you're really mean, ruining Oliver's shirt, Adam.' She looked at him, her eyes brimming with tears, then passed over him and fixed on Toby standing by the window.

'It was you, wasn't it?'

'Me? What?' Toby wore the blandest of expressions.

'Admit it.'

'Admit what, woman?'

'You, who did it, I mean, from up here, on Oliver.' She gave up her attempt at precision before the blank faces. 'We had such a nice evening together,' she said, plumping herself down on the bed and brushing her eyes with her sleeve. She lifted her knees so Adam could see her upper leg. At that moment Oliver entered, in his grey suit and striped Jermyn Street shirt. He stood in the middle of the room, looking at Toby and blinking heavily. 'Why did you do it, Toby? Was there any particular reason?'

'Do what?' Toby seemed tired of the whole business and Poppy and Mary were already discussing other subjects on the bed.

'He means that he suspects you peed on him from a height,' Mary said. 'Even if you didn't do it, why not apologise all the same?'

'I like that. Even though it was me who didn't do it, I have to apologise. What about you lot who discussed not doing it?'

Oliver had crossed his arms and was waiting for a satisfactory response.

'We're all very sorry for whatever happened or did not happen,' said Mary, patting the bed beside her for Oliver to sit down. 'Why don't we all have some nice heroin and forget this little *contretemps*.'

'No,' said Adam.

'Adam, don't fuss.' It was Mary who had spoken.

'No,' said Adam.

'You don't have to watch, if you don't like it.' Adam looked round the room. Oliver was blinking furiously behind a protective wall of females. Poppy was lying face down, her skirt riding down to her waist as her legs thumped up and down on the quilt. Toby had turned back to the window. Mary was smiling her queer half-smile. Adam walked from the room, shutting the door gently behind him.

In the hall, just inside the front door where Henry the butler had been taking names, Laura was standing and listening to a young man. Adam tried to slip by.

'Adam,' she said in surprise.

'A bit tired, that's all.'

'Adam, what's the matter? Do you know Adam Murray? William Smith.'

'Yes,' said Adam.

'I was telling tales of mine host at the Admiral,' said Smith.

'Excuse me. Air. Frightfully smoky, isn't it?'

'Oh Adam, what's going to happen there?'

'Excuse me. Just a breath of air. See you later, William. Log.'

'Don't call me that,' she hissed at his back.

Air. The flickering torches. Hydrangeas waving over the railings of the square garden, the same sort of thing in a way. Somebody is jumping up and down on a motorbike, demented.

'Toby, what are you doing? You were upstairs.' The face lifts the helmet, slashed at the base with a smile. It is not Toby but some demon sent to impersonate him. The trees in the square garden make a dark canopy over his head.

'Ah yes. Bloody thing. Could you very kindly give me a bump start? Oh, it's you, Adam.'

'Toby, where are you going? Whose bike is that?'

'Just round the square. You see, there's no slope. Otherwise, I could start it myself. Why don't you come? Sure to be another helmet somewhere. Going to Oddjob's man. As a peace offering.' He jumps up once again onto the kick start.

'Whose bike is that?'

'I imagine it's David's or somebody's. Had a key. How do you get second on this thing.' He is fighting with the levers on the handlebars.

'Pull that lever in first. That's it. Toby, you shouldn't do it. You're plastered. You'll wobble and fall off.'

'That must be second. Are you ready?' He puts his right foot on the foot-rest and turns the front wheel to avoid the hydrangeas.

The back of the seat is soft, the boots slip. So heavy at first to get over the camber. Then the exhaust fires at the shins and he is away around the square, running noisily through the gears, appears once in a small gap in the trees and then wobbles back into sight, passes, waves, and then just a red light winking in the shop windows of a side street.

The streets are empty. Adam's crooked step taps out in the darkness. The streets are strange and then familiar as he passes in and out of little areas where women he has known have lived and he has stayed, little patches of light like those cast by sodium street lamps, the newsagent where he buys cigarettes, the *DT* and the *Life* with a bad head or the Italian restaurant where they sat vacantly that evening.

Or is it the Corniche, with the sea on his left hand and the shuttered Lunapark ahead and the fires of rubbish where armed men warm themselves against the darkness? He comes at last within the largest circle of light, cast by

Clements Street, such a good part of London, like the room with a carpet in a boarding house or the wing of the Admiral that faces inwards.

Adam has no key and climbs in through a skylight in the garage, there where Toby used to store his things and the dead birds had hung so long.

Adam did not sleep, although he climbed the winding stair to Mary's bedroom. It was two o'clock but seemed to Adam later. He took everything out of his pockets and made a small pile on the floor under the desk. There was not much: notecase, Press card, the key he should have returned to Lydia, the stub of his train ticket from Exeter. The pile looked foolish on the floor so he put it in a drawer of Mary's dressing table; but, worried that he might forget the place in the morning, he cleared a space on top. Then he put it all back in his pocket and went downstairs.

He had an idea that he had put his passport in among his books but they were all jumbled up with Mary's and he could not find it. He started reorganising the books. He tried to summon a picture of the passport, its blue and gold lying beside or under something, in a pile of other things or peering out of some pocket. He moved to the dining room.

Adam was back upstairs when the telephone rang.

'Oh, Adam, it's you.' Mary was speaking over a babble of party sounds. 'Were you tired, poor thing? I suppose it was the journey up from home.'

Not tired. Tapping. Footsteps tapping.

'Look, my Habash. Has Toby ended up there?'

'No. Toby.' Adam thought hard. 'On a motorbike. A red light winking in the shop windows. He was going to.' Adam had forgotten the name.

'What? You're rambling. You're drunk.'

'Not drunk.'

'Well, if he comes, tell him he's in disgrace. He's got all our money.' She rang off.

Perhaps it was in the hall, in that little chest of drawers. No. Not there. Only Mary's rejected clothes. It must have fallen behind the cushions of the drawing-room sofa. That is where things usually were.

He was picking out coins and matchsticks from the back of the sofa when the telephone rang again. It was David.

'I'm bringing the girls home. Will you be up? Can you manage them?' His voice sounded curiously assured. Adam had not noticed the Midlands accent before.

'Up now.' David rang off.

The coats, of course. He was always wearing different coats. There were so many hanging by the front door and it would be a sensible place to carry a passport, where it would not put a suit out of shape.

No. Toby was born in Ireland. His mother lived in Galway. Do you need a passport for Ireland, too?

Perhaps in the garage. He was always putting things down there, for he needed two hands to get up through the skylight and he sometimes forgot to go back down. What a lot of Toby's stuff! Two trunks and a tea-chest and many cardboard boxes full of books and clothes. There must be a lifetime's worth here.

Toby always seemed temporary. His shirts so crumpled and his suits so ill-cared for, they seemed nothing more than housings, to be used for a day and then let fall to end up in boxes here; and books, these books, back through Oxford to the primers of Westminster and the Dragon, mere encumbrances to warp and fox in a tea chest.

Toby was always and only Toby. He was not a house or an old name or a book on the Palestinians or a sexual oddity or a first like Johnny but neither more nor less than what appeared, untidy but compact, fitting astride a motorbike or inside something.

A large car drew softly to a stop outside.

The two girls were in the back. Besides David in the front sat another man. Nobody stirred from within the car.

Adam walked round to David's window.

'Do you want me to come?'

'No, thank you very much. If you would kindly take Mary and Laura in.' David stared in front of him. The formality surprised Adam.

Smith got out of the car steadily, shook Adam's hand and

held open the door for the girls. Laura came out feet first. She had difficulty standing and her bag burst open, spilling chequebook, eye marker, hairbrush, papers.

'Did someone ring Ireland?'

'Yes, yes.'

'Will you be coming back?'

'We might have to,' said Smith. 'Don't wait up.'

Adam took Laura upstairs. She climbed straight into bed with her shoes on. Her blue eyes were quite blank. Adam reached under the bedclothes and took away her shoes, feeling her cold feet through holed nylon stockings. She looked at him as if about to speak and then closed her eyes as if a wave of something was breaking over her. She kept them shut and, after a while, Adam left the room, picking up his passport from her dressing table and closing the door gently behind him.

A little light was in the sky through the drawing-room window. Mary was wrapped in a coat, gulping whisky. Adam sat down beside her and put his arm round her back but she shivered and he removed it.

'It was on the way you know. Strawberry jam,' she said suddenly in her clear voice.

'Oh what does it matter now.' Adam bowed his head. She tapped him on the back.

'You know what I mean. I wouldn't mean that.' They settled into silence.

In bed, they lay as far apart as possible. The morning began to fill with small and obsessive sounds. Once Laura cried out: 'Johnny. Johnny,' and Adam went in to her but her eyes were tight shut. Adam did not sleep and dressed quickly when he heard the large, quiet car draw up.

'Where should it go?' David held a small parcel with care.

'I suppose in the garage for the moment.'

'Girls all right?' Smith asked.

'Asleep.'

'Oh Christ, let's have breakfast at Harry's.' Adam looked at David in surprise; but he did not want to be alone either.

They ate bacon and eggs behind a noisy group of Persian men. Music drifted their way from the piano. Adam wondered how anybody could dance at that time of the morning.

'It's a terrible lesson for us all,' David said, and then, as if the others had not understood: 'I mean this thing this evening. Drinking and driving.'

Adam looked up: 'Let's go.'

'Where?' Poor David, thought Adam.

'Out.'

David kindly paid the large cheque. In the hall, Adam and Smith glanced automatically at the Reuters tape machine. The story carried three bells but Adam was not at all surprised to learn that the Israel Defence Force had crossed in Lebanon.

TWO

CROSSING AT THE MUSEUM

CHAPTER EIGHT

Adam crossed at the Museum just after dawn.

The news in Damascus was bad. The crossings were all closed, they said; the Admiral had been hit and Boutros had fled; the correspondents had all left for Achrafiyeh on the eastern side. Adam believed none of it, but he set off after only an hour's wait, at midnight.

Adam had no choice. The airport shut down on the first day and he feared that if he went over by day, or if he stopped in Achrafiyeh, the Kataib might hold him again or he might not dare to cross. He had no money. He had gone to Bruton Street but Butterworth had given him only the air ticket and 200 Syrian pounds for the taxi to Beirut, all against the fee for the lecture. Adam had blustered about the siege economy and said that Johnny at least had cash in his pocket, which Smith had given him for the greyhound; but Butterworth looked blank and said he could borrow off Boutros like everybody else.

The driver was from Aleppo and did not speak much; or perhaps it was the sound of the bombardment, miles away over Adam's left shoulder, which inhibited them both as they hurried north. It sounded a little like heavy volumes falling from a bookshelf. They kept the windows open for the cool air and, by the time they reached Homs, the sound had stopped or been blocked by the hills.

(David had been a tower of strength, Toby's mother had said on the telephone from Ireland. So many friends and doing so well at the bank, she had said and caught her breath heavily. A waste, Adam had said and they had both fallen silent.)

'You will come with me to Aleppo,' the driver said shyly. 'My son came out of the city with the others.' He smiled

97

cleverly: 'With one small injury, thanks be to God. He will be your friend.'

'Thank you, you are kind. But go left here, to the border.' The driver took the left fork with a sigh. First light revealed grassy hills and the mass of Krak des Chevaliers on their right.

(The south fell even before David had arranged the air tickets and the car at Shannon. Adam thought all the way of Beaufort Castle and its sunburnt blocks of undressed stone tumbling down towards the Litani gorge, red poppies in spring and tumbleweed in the holes left by 150mm shells. He tried to imagine the blue Star of David on a white field hanging limply over the keep and military vehicles clogging the road north. Soon tour buses would be parked at the gatehouse and New York Jewish ladies would be shown, chattering, round the dungeons where this was done and that came to pass. Such a short time in the life of that old muddle of stone, so rough and futile and helpless, like poor Toby.)

The border guards were asleep on the oil-stained tarmac. The sergeant emerged from his blankets in pink, striped pyjamas. 'Could you please stamp my passport,' Adam said. His eyes were beginning to hurt with the light.

'Too much bomb bomb in Beirut,' the sergeant said, buttoning his uniform over his pyjamas. He blew on the stamp. 'Why don't you wait here and breakfast will be brought? For us, it is Ramadan.'

'Thank you. You are kind and I will return.' Adam looked round at dusty oleanders and the conscripts waking up to their fast. Beneath a collapsing acacia was a Lebanese taxi, its roof thick with white dust, its driver asleep in a cot. Upright on the back seat sat an old woman in white rags. Adam gave away half of Butterworth's money.

(A light drizzle was falling as David drove them up the little road north, past tiny irregular fields full of stones and modern bungalows with plots of windswept dahlias. The church was flinty and protestant. Adam stood outside to smoke a cigarette and let the rain blow into his face. The nave was crowded and a little woman tiptoed towards them and kissed Laura. The congregation talked ceaselessly in whispers, casting the occasional glance at their pew.)

As they approached Tripoli, the sounds of battle came out to meet them and made the old woman shriek, though whether from fear or some other emotion, Adam could not tell. There was fighting in Tripoli last year, too; there was always fighting in Tripoli. They drove onto the edge of the bay, where a row of shops opened out on a view of the town.

Adam looked up and saw white smoke rising from the apartment blocks which went up in steps up the hill. The woman turned wildly at him, then ruffled his hair: 'Israel,' she said and laughed. Adam helped her out of the car for she was blind.

(The path led through a little wicket and in steps up the hill. The wind had now got up and Adam felt himself breasting the gale, unable to move. Behind him, shrieks of good-natured panic and embarrassment were gusting about, hats off, skirts over heads.)

'It is your decision,' said the driver.

Adam got out of the car but butchers were pulling sheep into doorways and opening them up, while their apprentices unwound the entrails. Adam got back in the car.

'It's on the hill. Drive as fast as you can.'

(Laura was standing across the grave from him, looking down, her arm holding her dress down. She had taken off one shoe and her stocking was holed at the toe. She put her toe into the pile of earth. Something began to rattle on the wooden lid. Adam started to move round towards her but David caught her first and took her back.)

Jounieh was wide awake and the streets were full of young girls, all dressed in turquoise, which was that year's colour in France. They looked at Adam through the corner of their eyes then leaned on one another and smiled. The statue of the Virgin stood on the cliff over the Dog River. Adam marvelled that it had not been hit.

'We shall stop here,' the driver said. 'You can take your breakfast and admire these beautiful maids.'

'Thank you. But we must go to the Museum.' Adam leaned back and closed his eyes which hurt with the sunlight and the brown girls and their turquoise trousers.

(The little woman screamed but David held him back. Mary was white and her left arm hung limply. There was a little blood on the wrist and she was dribbling on the thick white carpet. He tried to reach Oliver but David held his arms. Afterwards, Mary was sick and Adam apologized to the little woman.)

'Do you speak French?' Adam woke up. A face was staring at him closely. Behind was the pitted portico of the Museum.

'I was asleep.' The Kataib officer took his passport. He had an uneasy motion of his left shoulder but looked neat in his Israeli uniform, which carried a red epaulette marked Security. 'I'm a journalist going to my office in the city.'

'The admiral, I suppose,' said the officer. 'You won't find anybody there but criminals. Everybody is working from this side. ABC, NBC, Stern, Christian Monitor.' He handed Adam back his passport. 'Haven't I seen you before?'

'Maybe. Can we take the car?'

'No.'

Adam looked down the wide street to the red earthworks at its end, shimmering a little in the heat. The crossing was empty. 'Why is nobody on the crossing?'

'Don't ask me. Ask them.' The officer laughed and strolled back to his comrades under the portico of the Museum. Adam gave away the rest of Butterworth's money.

(This is how it begins, crossing at the Museum. Last year, blue jacarandas were in flower, but these trees are orange-red, Persian acacia, perhaps, Lydia would know, with sprigs of red flowers; past the Palais Mansour, where Parliament used to meet when it was safe; my back is wide, my chest is wide; past the Palais de Justice; I carry a typewriter and Toby's Revelation suitcase; past the crenellated wall of the French Ambassador's castle of a Residence, with the tricolor still floating through the busted pines; past the Hippodrome, which was bombed on the first day.)

'Stop.' A boy stepped out from behind the red earth rampart so that his AK swung and pointed at Adam's chest. A dog of indeterminate breed but with a spiked collar was urinating on the earthwork.

'Hello, sweet youth. I am a journalist going to my office in the city.'

'Welcome,' said the boy, taking Adam's passport. He did not attempt to read it. On his upper arm was a crudely cut piece of red linen, stamped in Arabic: Higher Security Committee of the Joint Forces. The boy smiled most sweetly. 'But you have no passport from our allies, the Palestine Liberation Organisation.'

Adam looked again at the epaulette. It must have been copied through binoculars, the very best he could do. The dog was showing its teeth. 'My dear, you expect more than I can give. I have only just come from London over Damascus and Tripoli.'

'What news from Tripoli?'

'There were incidents, mortars and RPG, just after dawn when we passed through. What news here?'

'Quiet. Bad yesterday. From the air, the sea and the hill.'

An officer called sharply from under the red trees.

'Will you come back to visit us,' the boy said quickly, straightening in military fashion. The dog was snarling now. 'The other correspondents speak English. I think for many of them, Arabic is difficult, Mr Adam.'

'How did you know my name?' The officer had stood up and was coming towards them. He had curly hair and was stockily built like Toby. The boy turned away.

'Give me your name,' Adam said. 'Just one name. So I know.'

'Omar. Go now.'

Adam threaded the slalom of earthworks, watched by the officer and the dog.

'Hello, Boutros,' said Adam in English. The proprietor of the Admiral Hotel was seated, despite the early hour, suited but tieless, in the same green armchair he had occupied since the Civil War or, at least, as long as Adam remembered. The windows had been crudely taped and the swimming pool seemed to have no water in it.

Mr Boutros Wazzan, proprietor of the Admiral Hotel and sundry other properties of greater significance, turned round, recognised Adam, stood up and, then, tried to find the name.

'It's Adam Murray. *DT*. I was here last year. Have you got a room?'

'Of course, I haven't got a room.' He looked Adam up and down and laughed. 'You're a bit late, aren't you? Fuad,' he shouted, galvanising the front desk into action. 'Give Murray a room on the first floor. 109. That's the worst I've got. Not quite high enough to be safe from car bombs.' He laughed again. 'I suppose you want some bloody money, too?'

Adam nodded.

'Fuad'll give you a thousand dollars. Might last you a day. Have some breakfast. We're not fasting.'

'Who's here, Boutros?' The coffee was strong and sweet.

'The usual riff-raff and terrorist sympathisers. I kicked the French out, didn't I, Fuad,' he raised his voice to reach the front desk, then turned sharply on Adam. He was trembling a little. 'Look, I don't want a repetition of that incident last year. The situation is much worse now, you know? You'll be out on your ear.'

'No, no, Boutros, it won't happen again. I was drunk and frightened. You know how it is.' Adam felt contrite although what the incident had been, or whether he had, in fact, been involved in it, whatever it was, he did not know.

Room 109 would take some time to make up (or, as Adam suspected, to evict its occupant) for many of the regular staff had fled and Boutros was relying on refugees from the south who were willing but, well, not very experienced. There was no mains power at all but Boutros had fuel-oil for the generator for seven days. The Israelis had, it seemed, cut the mains power, and the central telephone exchange down at Riad Solh was running on batteries, which were being recharged. Arafat had ostentatiously put men round the building, Boutros said, and if Murray wanted to compete with the networks he might get a telephone line one day. It could have been worse.

Adam wandered out of the main door and sat down on the edge of a dry flower bed. The streets were full of people making hurried purchases from the shopkeepers who had raised their blinds a few feet. In place of the usual hotel drivers and their agents sat four armed men in tee-shirts advertising American publications.

'Hello,' said Adam.

'Hello,' said their leader or spokesman, whose fat belly was clad in a tee-shirt marked *Newsweek*. *Do not shoot. Ne Tirez Pas* and then the Arabic word for Press underneath. He leaned his AK-47 against the wall and walked over to Adam.

'Are you responsible for the overall security of this building?' Adam asked helpfully.

'That is correct! I am the Captain and these are the warriors.'

'Welcome,' said Adam.

'Welcome,' said the captain of the guard.

'Mister Adam. Mister Adam.' The warriors woke from their torpor and unhitched their rifles. Adam got up and there, under a box tree, beside his spotless red Chevrolet, was Said, worst of drivers.

'Said,' Adam said, embracing the tall young man. He looked well, thinner, but with the same pressed jeans and French tee-shirt. 'How are you? How is your colour? How is your household? How is your car? How is the war? Are you married? Have you children? How are you?'

'So you have come back,' said Said, standing back and looking angrily at Adam. 'I heard this but I did not believe it, because it was such a blessing. I said you would not come back because of the war. You are wise, I said.'

'Do you have work, dear Said?'

'Too much work. NBC. Every day 1,000 liras. But they are not as you are. Friendship has no price.'

Adam thought of Butterworth in Bruton Street. '500 liras for me every day.'

Said turned away and put his arms on the roof of his beautiful car. He shook his head slowly. 'Friendship has no price.'

'Come on, Said.' Adam had not realized how much he had relied on finding him. 'How much are you paying for benzine.'

'30 liras a litre, unless my father brings it from Achrafiyeh and that is risky because the Kataib might not let him across.' He turned and there were tears in his eyes.

'All right, 600 liras to begin with. We will decide at the end. And you must take me where I ask, unless you fear for the beautiful car and when you leave me in a bad place you must watch me in the street and then wait for me to return. And if you see someone watching me you must watch him and then tell me.'

'I cannot do it.' Said shook his head and opened the door.

'For a start, let's go to Verdun and then down to Fakhani to see the PLO. The ceasefire might not last.'

Said rolled back the roof and smiled in the sunlight. 'Too much cluster in the streets. It was bad yesterday.'

'Then drive slowly,' said Adam: but Said did not, sending the great car thundering through the checkpoints on Rue Verdun, though it did not matter for the Syrian soldiers had gone.

'Why did you stay, Said, if your family is in Achrafiyeh?'

'Business,' said Said and smiled modestly. 'It is expensive for them there. Anyway, this is my home.'

Adam found the Research Institute with difficulty, but a boy jumped up unslinging his rifle when they tried to park.

'Car bombs. You must walk,' said Said. The boy wore a baby blue tee-shirt and a bead necklace. He was very tense.

'Hello, I have come to see Mr Sarabi. I am a journalist.'

'Not here.' Behind the boy, through the open door of the institute, Adam saw scenes of strange domesticity, women and cooking pots and dirty children. 'Not here, you understand.' Refugees they must be, from the camps in the south taking most of the fire. Something was wrong.

'Not here,' said the boy again, looking at Adam carefully. 'I think maybe I have seen you before.'

'Maybe.'

As Said turned off Corniche Mazraa into the Palestinian suburbs, Adam sensed a change. The streets were empty of people except boys in uniform, wandering in pairs. The only vehicles were military, plastered all over with red mud. 'Very bad yesterday down here,' said Said, guessing his thoughts. 'From the air, the sea and the land. Fakhani, Sabra, Chatila and Borj al-Brajnie; many people killed. All day.'

'Ah, Said. I wonder, have you seen any Europeans down here? Apart from journalists and doctors? When you came with NBC?'

'No,' Said said thoughtfully. 'Turks, yes, Kurds, Indians, Bangladesh. English, no.'

'Not English, necessarily.'

They stopped at a checkpoint where a broken stand-pipe was gushing water but the guard shouted excitedly through Adam's window: 'Quick. He is at the office. Go quickly.'

'You are lucky,' said Said as they hurried on. 'First day.' But as Adam got out of the car, he felt his nerve give. Glass crunched under his feet and, behind a knot of people standing in front of the entrance to the Arab University, an eight-storey building had collapsed. The lower floors leaned at 45-degree angles and everywhere twisted metal stuck out to pierce or masonry seemed poised to fall and crush. It was deathly still but for the sound of feet on glass as Adam tiptoed towards the little crowd.

He was speaking quickly in English, gesturing occasionally to the ruined building behind him, while Hassan translated into French and German. He wore a forage cap in place of his usual headscarf but his eyes still sparkled in the way Adam remembered. He smiled all the time as if he alone understood the meaning of all these sharp and heavy things. This is a war of genocide, look, he said. We will not leave here, except to Palestine. Let them come and try to kill us. They shall find us waiting.

A cameraman slipped out to change his film cassette and Adam found himself face to face with him. He wore, Adam noticed as he looked down and prepared his question, elastic-sided boots and he smelt vaguely of good soap.

'Abu Ammar,' said Adam.

'Abu Ammar,' said Hassan, first with French and then with German intonation.

'Don't you think that the time . . .'

'N'y a-t-il pas une chance . . .'

'Glauben Sie nicht, dass es eine Gelegenheit gibt . . .'

'To consolidate,' Adam went on, flustered. 'You suffer appalling losses without political gain. Is it not time to end the Beirut phase?'

He interrupted the translation. 'You ought to be ashamed of yourself,' he sparkled at Adam.

'Ashamed of yourself,' he repeated and Adam could feel the journalists writing it down for a second time.

'*Schaemst du dich nicht . . .*'

'To sacrifice the heroic efforts of the Palestinian and Lebanese masses for,' he gestured at the building, 'for what? We are going nowhere but Palestine.' He turned with disgust to another questioner.

'Poor old Murray,' said Hassan, putting his arm round Adam's shoulder and watching his leader depart, whisked off in a car, to God knows where. 'Always putting your foot in it. Don't take it to heart. It was mainly for TV.'

'I know,' said Adam, though he felt mortified.

'What can I do for you, anyway?' Hassan said as they walked towards his office. He pointed to a row of shell canisters lined against the wall. 'Seen these? Cluster shells and bombs. Very nice. A gift from our American cousins.'

'I was going to ask for another interview with the great man but I think I might wait. Do I have to have a pass?'

'Why not?' The office had been moved from the first floor to the basement, which was dark and had none of the revolutionary posters Adam remembered from upstairs. There was a telex machine, Adam noted automatically, and several men, some armed, sitting quite silently.

'Oh and Hassan . . .' Adam said as softly as he could. It was as if the room contained a new corpse. Hassan had sat down at the telex machine and was staring, preoccupied, at the keyboard as if he expected it suddenly to spring to life.

'Hassan, I thought I might do a piece about people fighting with the Joint Forces out of conviction. You know, non-Palestinian or other Arabs. Any ideas?'

Hassan turned round and looked carefully at Adam. 'We don't fight for fun, you know. Watch it, lad. Adwan will give you a pass for five days.'

Adam sat in intense discomfort as Adwan made out the

pass in his careful, slow hand. Adam read it over his shoulder. 'The Information Director of the Palestine Liberation Organisation requests all military . . .'

Hassan was still hunched over the telex machine as if he felt, at that very moment, an operator in the State Department was punching a tape that implied some role in the future for his shattered organisation. Adam thanked Adwan and turned furtively to leave.

'Murray,' Hassan snapped without looking up. 'You can't travel through these areas without an escort. Otherwise,' he looked up and smiled wearily, 'we can't be responsible for your safety. I mean it, Murray.'

'Got you, Hassan. Thanks.' Adam walked out into the sunlight and dropped to his knees as the ruined building began to settle in on itself.

Adam moved his things into his room and had lunch downstairs, although he had no appetite. The Admiral's dining-room had come to resemble a sergeants' mess. A trestle table supported a buffet of Eggins-like unsuitability – curry, sweet and sour pork, huge and uneven steaks – while journalists in their equivalent of combat uniform picked at their plates or tuned their little radios to Kol Israel.

Out in the bright sunlight, Adam could not find Said. The captain of the guard sidled over and hinted that he had information to the effect that Said had gone off in search of benzine but would return in not more than five minutes. Adam could feel his story taking shape and set off to Reuters on foot.

It was not too bad. It could have been so much worse, he thought, walking nice and slow down past the Narodny Bank, not catching anybody's eye but answering civilly if men with guns questioned him, stopping by the abandoned Information Ministry to talk to the Kurdish stallholders to see what fruit and vegetables they had and what they were running out of because of the blockade. He came to the Prime Minister's office and the row of closed plywood shops running down through Sanaya Garden. He thought of Laura's house in Scotland. It would not take long, he thought, if the ceasefire held and the Americans kept them from coming into the city.

There was a girl in the street with a striped tee-shirt like Said's and the loveliest, long black hair Adam had ever seen. She had a bandage on her left wrist. Adam quickened his step so he could overtake her and see her face and then a big hand picked him off his feet and he was tumbling head first towards her, on into the plywood shops under the park trees, except she was turning over and her legs were in the air. Oh my darling, I've been hit, shot in my wide back.

Adam crashed into the side of the girl's belly.

'*Um Gottes Willen*,' she said, spitting all over his neck.

'Please walk, quickly.'

'But my duty . . .'

He pushed her forward at an embarrassed half-run. Gunfire erupted on both sides of the garden and then a second explosion sent them sprawling forward. Adam could see the antique column in the little roundabout in front of Reuters but the gunfire seemed to be coming down all the streets towards them. The girl was dazed; she was trying to crawl back from where they had come. These shops will not stop anything, Adam thought, and looked up to the balcony of Reuters and saw somebody he had not expected to see, head below the stone balustrade, body compact and tense and military behind a steel water tank.

'Hold onto the girl,' Smith shouted cleanly and slowly. 'Go back ten yards and take a good run up. No, keep hold of her. Now run and upright this time.'

Run upright: that is what Lukomski had said. The only thing that matters is speed. Once in the fire zone, he had said, the chances of a stray bullet are constant. What can be reduced, he had said, is the target.

Adam propelled the girl into the dark hall of the Reuters building and crouched down behind a chipped stone lion. The fire was panic, of course; still, not too bad.

'Hello, ah, William,' Adam said, looking up at the head through the balustrade. Adam heard a siren; an ambulance, no doubt, or perhaps there might even be a fire engine left.

'Hello. We heard you were coming. You've torn your shirt and your elbow is bleeding, not very badly.'

Adam found it hard to reach his elbow. He tried one way, and then the other, and then examined the shirt Mary had given him. It was a good shirt. He tried to put the torn pieces together to make the sleeve whole. Then he picked out small pebbles from the bloody section.

'Where were they?' Smith reduced his size once again as the first ambulance went by, with gunmen hanging on to the outside and firing in the air to clear the traffic, although there was none.

'What? The explosions? Behind me.'

'These car bombs are getting on my nerves.'

'Oh, William. We had better go, hadn't we?'

'I think I might give this one a miss. I went down for the big one at the Phoenicia.'

'Isn't it our duty?' What a strange thing to say, Adam thought.

'But, old boy, there might be one more. The second one at the Phoenicia would have done for us all if the local creeps hadn't driven it off by accident. We should wait a bit.'

Adam walked into the dark hall, but among the refugee families huddled against the walls he could not find the girl. Smith emerged on the stairs and was immediately set upon by children. Adam hardly recognized him. His short hair was recently washed and his safari suit pressed; but his eyes were half-closed and he moved with care and deliberation as they set off along the doorways of the street. An ambulance shrieked down towards them but, as far as Adam could see through the open back doors, empty.

As they moved along the row of shops, a boy ran out into the little square in front of the Prime Minister's office and raised his rifle. Adam and Smith lay on the ground.

'No fire discipline,' said Smith, as half a magazine passed over their heads. 'Bloody rear-echelon rabble. Still, it'll keep your mind off your friend. I'm terribly sorry about that.'

'A waste,' said Adam. The boy had put down his rifle.

'You ought to see to your arm if you don't have to file.'

'I think I'd better get off the mark. The *DT* can't make up its mind if it's interested in the story. That's why they won't send a staffer.' The boy was still standing in the middle of the road.

'Could you speak to that loon, please?'

Adam got up carefully, hands away from his side, approached the boy, shook his hand and explained they were journalists. The boy took them on.

'Any news of Johnny Penrose?' They had reached the place where Adam had fallen and he could feel the heat of the fire.

'Who?' said Smith, without hesitation. 'Is he a hack?'

'We were at Oxford together,' Adam said quickly. Then he turned the corner and the heat came out like a bare fist and shut him up.

He had expected the fire, in what might once have been cars, and perhaps also the glass all over the street; but the leaves blasted off the box-trees that deadened their tread or the pieces of greyish flesh that hung in the branches or had stuck to the white walls and the shoes of the gunmen and orderlies? And the smell of something roasting like some unspeakable barbecue?

Adam turned away because of the heat from the fire.

A dazed dresser walked between them, so close that he brushed Adam's chest. He was carrying something in paper in his hand.

'Oh my God? *Lahm al-insani*?' The dresser looked right past Adam.

'It is half a foot, or to be exact, the musculature of a foot.' William Smith spoke carefully and clearly as if the boy would understand. 'Excuse me, how many casualties are there?'

Adam translated. 'How can I know?' the boy said. 'At least four dead. More, maybe, in the offices.' He turned his blank eyes on Adam. 'Your elbow is bleeding, not seriously,' he said.

Adam turned away because of the heat of the fire. Up the street, ripe tomatoes were rolling slowly down towards them; beside the overturned barrow, a girl in a white coat and with very long black hair was tending a man's face. Adam took a step towards her and then jumped back because someone was firing over his head.

'All journalists leaving! No photograph taking!' The man was very short and frightened.

'My dear,' said Adam soothingly. 'We are doing our work only.'

'All journalists leaving!' Something hit Adam painfully on the shin. He glanced down and the tarmac was splintering at his feet. He screamed and jumped in the air and Smith pulled him away.

'Why do they do that?' Adam asked as they set off back through the plywood shops. 'I mean fire at our feet. Without us, they'd be even worse off.' An untidy group of women and children was drifting out of Sanaya Garden to form a silent knot in the road.

'They're frightened, aren't they? They're keeping order, aren't they?'

Children clutched at their upper legs and old women looked at them shyly.

'So, you haven't seen Penrose?' Adam gently unhitched the children for his legs were losing their strength.

'He's not a hack, is he?' Again, there was no hesitation.

'No, I wouldn't have thought so. He was at the Palestine Research Institute?'

'Well, that's completely finished. It's full of refugees from Borj al-Brajnie.'

'Have you or anyone seen Sarabi? Is he in uniform again?'

'Ah,' said Smith, stopping. 'Look, I wouldn't mention his name if I were you. There's a rumour going round that he's been held.'

'What did Hassan say? What did Hassan say?'

'Not confirm or deny. Waste of time.'

Adam turned away and leaned against a shop. 'I'm sorry, William. I'm having difficulty walking. Those car bombs rather take it out of one.' The dark hall of Reuters beckoned across the roundabout, beyond the Greco-Roman column in the middle.

'Come on. You can manage. Hard cheese. First day.' Adam did, climbed the steps into the dark hall, disentwined more children and, behind Reuters' unshiverable perspex windows, allowed his arm to be bound by one of the telex operators, with a sheet of paper torn from a fresh roll.

Adam joined a group clustered round the radio. The newsreader was a girl with a musical voice and Frenchified Arabic.

'How much are they telling?' asked Smith.

'25 and 20 kilograms and the car number-plates,' said Adam. 'Oh yes, and the first went off seconds after Arafat passed in a car.'

'Scum,' said Smith.

'William, that's not definite evidence. You can't pin it on the Kataib.'

'Scum.'

Adam's story flowed without interruption and he looked up, at the last take, to see Said pretending to be angry. He handed Adam three cartons of cigarettes. 'They said you might be here.'

'Let's go, Said. There was a bomb. Did you get benzine?'

'Yes. Some crazies came and shot out one man's tyres. They said it was now a military petrol station. But I waited and then the explosions came and they drove away. 35 liras a litre.'

'Oh Said, well done. And the cigarettes.' Adam walked out to look for Smith but he was fast asleep in the telex room. 'Said,' said Adam, as he got into the car. The back seat was piled high with cigarette cartons. It was getting dark. 'Look Said, can you get me some drugs?'

'Of course. Some of the fighters smoke hashish before an action. It helps them forget their fear.'

'Yes, that is true and would be good. But can you get me some heroin?'

'Of course,' said Said and looked at Adam curiously. The street in front of the Prime Minister's office was blocked off. 'Fucking bomb people,' he said. 'I can get that for you, if you want it, although it is not so safe.'

'Language, Said! Whatever you think.' Adam felt exhausted.

'I think beer is better in a bad security situation.' He stopped the car by the Bristol and they went in and drank a tin of beer together and then another and rebound Adam's arm with paper napkins.

'No good heroin,' said Said, dropping Adam off at the

Admiral. It was almost night and, from the south of the town, the sound of artillery could be heard.

Boutros Wazzan, proprietor of the Admiral Hotel and sundry other properties, was dressing down the captain of the guard. 'So you're the new head of the Beirut Fire Department,' he said, gripping Adam's arm and gesturing at the big red car vanishing up the street.

'I love that boy.' Adam's legs were giving way.

'Yes. He's a good one. If anyone can keep you out of trouble, he will.'

An explosion made them drop to their knees. They looked at each other sheepishly, each with a hand on the door handle. 'What the hell was that?'

'That was your ceasefire,' said Boutros Wazzan. He put his arm round Adam and they went in.

CHAPTER NINE

The ceasefire survived for a while. This meant little to Adam for the bombardment of the southern suburbs never quite let up and the hospitals seemed always stretched to their limit, with orderlies running out to unload bleeding fighters or keening old women from the Volkswagen ambulances. Meanwhile, Palestinians negotiated with Lebanese, and Lebanese with Americans, and Americans with Israelis.

The Admiral had lost what little decorum it had once possessed. By night, the correspondents snarled and roared like wild beasts round the dry swimming pool and even a few rounds of automatic fire over the wall would not shut them up. One jumped into the swimming pool and broke his ankles; a second was pinioned by Smith before he could dive, weeping, in to save him.

It was as if, by staying up, they could keep the night and the aircraft away. Exactly at midnight, the sky over Borj al-Brajnie would shine with starshell or parachute flares which hung, breathtakingly deft and arrogant, just out of reach of the anti-aircraft fire and its last cooling tracer. Twice Adam woke to find himself on the floor, blown out of bed by an explosion that still reverberated, bright red, in his dreaming; but it was only a Phantom breaking the sound barrier a hundred feet overhead.

The days were not much better. Adam saw fear in every-thing: in unbroken sheets of glass or twisted billets of steel, among the refugee children playing in Sanaya Garden or in the ordure burning untended in the streets. Above all, Adam saw parked cars. All down the street were parked cars. In every street.

The captain of the guard followed Adam's gaze and loped

over to him. 'I have made a thorough check of all parked vehicles in the area under my responsibility. Do not be worried.'

Adam nodded but Said had emerged from somewhere, was standing behind the captain, and so he kept him all morning as they crossed and re-crossed the city, from Hassan's office to M. Le Président's book-lined cell, looking for information on the serpentine negotiations. In the car, absurdly, he felt safer.

Exactly at noon, two aircraft came in low from over the sea, disgorging pink smoke, then pink confetti and then pink leaflets which Adam had to jump to catch in the hot, draughty street. The Arabic was so queer that Said did not at first understand what the Israel Defence Force was threatening; but a man ran up to them, tore the leaflet from his hand, glanced at it and them, then ran for his car. They followed him to the Museum which was a solid line of overheating cars going out. There was no sign of Omar.

'Ah Said,' said Adam as they got back into the big red car. 'Let me ask you a question. How would you take something from this side to that side but secretly?'

'What, to smuggle food into Achrafiyeh?' Said seemed to find the notion extremely funny.

'No. I am not a fool. The Kataib are not fighting. Israel does their work for them. All right, maybe they set car bombs, maybe not. Their radio tells where the Palestinians have weapons, although I think Israel knows that already. All the Kataib need to do is sit at the Museum, the port and Galerie Semaan and stop things and people they do not like. Tell me of another place.'

'Go through the Museum.' Said started the engine. 'There is no problem for you. You are English. This is not your fight. The Museum is best.'

'Tell me of another place.'

'I do not know.'

'What about the Place des Canons?'

'Sharpshooters.'

'Well, let's look at the port.'

Said turned to the right and followed the hill down

towards the sea. Adam thought he must be angry for he drove fast and without care down the Green Line. The houses were battered and pitted and, occasionally, barricades had been erected lest this division of the city and the mind lose its form. Even the barricades had a permanent air about them. Adam closed his eyes and when he opened them again, they had come to the old commercial quarter.

It had rotted away. The streets Adam remembered from the first year with Johnny, Rue Weygand or Rue Leclerc with their shipping offices and warehouses, had lost their shape, were little more than slabs of red and sculpted earth sprouting wild figs and fireweed, relics of another battle. On the seafront, a hill of rubbish was burning as it had for as long as Adam remembered.

The fighting had begun in 197–, at the Place, then crawled down to the sea consuming brokers and freight forwarders and all their flour and fruit and rope, emerged at the Corniche, smelt the sea and sprang for the Holiday Inn till Sarabi beat it back and it retired, hissing, to coil itself among the ruins. A single street lived; but by day, achieving the atrocious gaiety of midnight only at noon. Women sat, painted, wigged, legs apart, on stools before curtained booths while drunken makeshifts reeled from door to door or slapped the roof of the car as Said picked his way carefully down the street.

A good, safe street, Adam thought. These must be deserters, Christian and Muslim, from the militias of either side; he could bring him here, if it got bad, shielded by drink and women for there is no day here but bright night and dark night and these are ruins of another battle. Said was embarrassed and drove straight through to the last checkpoint on their side, a blockhouse manned by two men with maroon berets.

'Liberation Army,' said Said. 'The Syrians left them behind to die.'

Adam got out of the car and showed himself to the two men. Through the slit in the pitted blockhouse, their eyes looked wild. Hash, thought Adam; or maybe it is just the place. It would take several visits, he thought, before they agreed to take him to the Place. He opened his mouth to greet them but they were looking not at him but at something over his shoulder. He glanced back up the street towards the Place and saw a man step out from behind a red earth barricade. He wore no shirt and his hair was white as brickdust. Oddly, his rifle was the American M-16.

Here, thought Adam. Here, of all places, in the ruins of a forgotten battle. 'Said, Said.'

The man brought his arm down. Adam dived for the car and as he landed in the back seat, he felt two rounds slap into the boot and half-spin the car round as Said reversed it, whining, towards the street of whores. The Palestine Liberation Army men did not fire their weapons.

Once through the women and deserters, Said turned the car round and parked on the sea front.

'I'm really sorry, Said. I'll pay for it.'

Said was angrily examining the damage. They opened the boot and found the two spent rounds. It could have been worse.

'No. The car is my responsibility.' Adam looked round and sniffed the sea air. The place looked changed. He wondered who was now in the Holiday Inn. There was a large crater on the Corniche itself.

'What's this, Said?' It was an immense hole, at least thirty feet deep and fifty across, and the sea water had seeped into the bottom. Said joined him on the rim.

'That was the big bomb. They said that when it exploded, houses, furniture, people went spinning into the sea. The windows broke in Hamra.' Adam looked round and all the houses that he now remembered had gone, down to their very foundations.

'I came down with Mr Smith immediately but the crazies were shooting and then there was another in a lorry which they found and drove away and it blew up beside the Holiday.'

'Let's get out of here, Said.'

Said looked at Adam carefully. 'I do not understand what you want. There is another place. Sodeco. But we need an armed element.'

'Whatever you think.'

They retraced their journey along the Green Line but this

time Said halted before a ruined building with a crude red-white-and-black flag for a door. It was an office of the Murabitoun. Adam's heart sank, for of all Ras Beirut militias these were the least confidence-inspiring; but a young boy with a beard emerged from behind the door curtain and embraced Said with respect.

He was so shy that at first he would not enter the car and then asked Adam if he were permitted to bring his rifle. Adam supposed he was some relation of Said's.

'My dear,' said Adam over his shoulder. 'I am writing an article for my newspaper on the blockade of the city. Show me the place where food and oil come over.'

'No oil,' he said. 'That is too dangerous.'

Said parked well back from the line and the boy took Adam forward. Great piles of red earth stood before the ruined houses, as if this part of the city had given up the pain of being a city and reverted to country. The only living things were lizards.

'Here is the place.'

It was an alley between two ruined lines of flats, closed at the end with a barricade of corrugated iron and masonry. Not an alley, really, thought Adam, but the courtyard of a low apartment block. Just to the right of the barricade and beyond it was half a two-storey house, the lost wall revealing a cornice and flowered wallpaper and the graffiti of the old East Beirut street gangs which had either been liquidated or absorbed, painfully, into the Kataib. Then Adam trembled for he seemed to be looking into a mirror.

'What is this place? Why do you show me this place?'

'There are, how do you say, relations.' The boy smiled shyly.

(This is how it had begun. He had been reading the graffiti and Lukomski was chivvying him along; but the graffiti were so revealing: Liban Sourire; Make love not war; An hour of war is better than a lifetime of peace. He had looked up to the end of the alley, to the point where he and the boy were today crouching, and seen a man on his haunches. His uniform was tight across his back, so tight there was no crease. Under his right epaulette was a maroon beret.)

'What do you mean, relations? I thought the Liberation Army was here.'

'No. This is our sector. They used to come before, to help, when there were incidents. But now they stay away, because they are weak now the Syrians have left.'

(Incidents. Accidents. The man with the maroon beret was peeing and he seemed to feel Adam's gaze through his creaseless back for he turned and their eyes crossed and Adam felt it might take some time for them to uncross. He fired twice, over the house, without getting up from his squat.)

'I do not understand. Last year, who was here? Who was here when the journalist died on the other side?'

'I do not know.' The boy reached out to capture a lizard but it scurried into a crack in the concrete. 'They came in the morning. They said they had warning the fascists were going to launch incidents in this sector. We had no warning for we have relations. They had one sharpshooter.'

('You dumb asshole! I told you about eye contact.' Lukomski pushed him down the stairs. The little Kataib guide had begun to shiver. Lukomski took the boy's M-16 from him and started telling Adam what to do but Adam was listening to the first returning fire out of their side. He was looking at the open space before them, which was flat and curiously free of weeds. He could just make out the marks of goal lines and penalty boxes. At the end was a row of overturned buses. He tried to listen to Lukomski but he kept looking at the buses and then down at his feet. Then a rocket-propelled grenade hit the building.)

'I do not like this place. It has a bad air.'

The boy nodded. 'We do not have another place.'

'Oh my dear, I did not mean that. I would not mean that.' Adam gave up. They scrabbled back to Said and the car.

In the course of the week, Adam regained some of his nerve. He took to walking again. He and Said became very prudent. Even in Ras Beirut, the siege had broken down last year's alliances, areas were changing control and every day there was some sort of battle for a street corner or a petrol station or a building in which to lodge refugees. Adam and

Said learned to avoid certain places and they did not return to the port or attempt again to penetrate the empty, rotted streets towards the Place des Canons.

In several respects, Adam felt more secure in the south of the town, at the front beyond Borj al-Brajnie or beside the airport and the Faculty of Sciences, although the dour exchanges of fire, shelling from the hills and rockets from the town, seemed to be increasing in volume and duration as if both sides were victims of a habituating drug. Yet the fighters at the front were better trained and were pleased that Adam had taken the risk to visit them. Also he was looking for Omar whom he did not think would be in the rear.

At first, Adam took Hassan's advice and warning seriously but the young escorts he brought from Fakhani put the fighters on edge. Their political lectures bored the young men as much as they bored Adam and they said things about the negotiations which he knew, from brisk encounters with the Prime Minister or the elegant architecture of M. Le Président's French, to be untrue. Instead, Adam and Said would go down alone and while Adam sat with the young men, Said would squander scarce water beautifying his car.

Omar had been moved from the Museum to a front in the south. It took three visits and hours under the red trees to establish that, for his former comrades at first did not recognise the name and, well, they all had smiles for a responsible journalist. They were mostly Mourabitoun, the very poorest of the West Beirut poor who had allied themselves with the Palestinians, out of the sympathy of the wretched and to improve their standing against the forces of the old Lebanon, and above all the Christians. They were now reaping, in varying degrees of anxiety and regret, their reward.

Their culture was of the simplest. Some wore cowboy hats they had seen in Italian western films before the Hamra cinemas had filled up with ammunition and refugees. Adam could not but visit them for he had little else to do. The *DT* was losing what little enthusiasm it had had for the story and the playbacks that arrived, irregularly, at Reuters indicated that his efforts were now running on inside pages and in abbreviated form.

In this he was no luckier than Smith who seemed scarcely to stir from the hotel except for some appalling act of daring in the waste ground by the Faculty of Sciences which left him no less moody and withdrawn and contemptuous of the boys risking a sniper's bullet to accompany him.

Said did not seem to mind these long waits under the red trees. He was always up to something. The year before, when they had been able to leave the city, Adam could never return to the car without Said showing off some purchase, the best cheese from Zahleh or peaches off the trees in the Chouf.

This year there was little to buy or sell and, anyway, Said's family was still in Achrafiyeh, complaining of the famine prices and the rapacious Greek-Catholic merchants and threatening to return. None the less, Said was always huddling in corners with the Museum fighters or disappearing into the bombed Hippodrome to seal some agreement, whither the officer would not permit Adam to follow him. Adam did not like the officer. He was as burly as Toby and had the air of a commissar. When not threatening the motorists trying to get back into the city, he would call Adam over for a lecture.

'Now, Mr Adam, I wish to show you the Higher Security Committee's Explosives Detection Unit.' He pointed with his rifle at the dog with the spiked collar.

'This animal is well trained,' the commissar said cautiously. The dog was perched on a rampart, urinating. 'He is trained to find hexagene and father of explosion in incoming cars. What is father of explosion, please?'

'TNT?' Adam felt tired and dispirited.

'Correct. TNT. Thank you.' The dog, its work done, was now snarling at the officer, who prudently stepped back under a tree. The dog took several steps towards them, showing his teeth. The man waved his rifle. The dog took another step towards them; then the man lost his head. He fired four rounds into the air. Adam jumped back as leaves and red flowers drifted down around him but the dog bounded straight in for the officer's groin.

Adam weighed in, found the dog's collar and sent him away with a kick but the damage, in the form of a torn uniform and a deep graze, was done. The officer sat up, reached out for his rifle and looked at Adam evilly. Adam stared out at the fighters under the trees by the Hippodrome and at the shimmering line of cars. Don't laugh; please don't laugh, he said to himself. 'Let us take you to the hospital,' he said, offering the officer his hand. 'That is a bad wound.'

The officer raised himself, unaided and with surprising agility. 'Thank you. We have our own medical stations to relieve pressure on civilian facilities. Now, you must leave. Your presence disturbs our important work.'

'Of course. Thank you.' Said was standing with the men at the entrance to the Hippodrome. His face was in shade but he did not seem to be smiling. The line of cars was silent. Adam felt like weeping.

As they drove into Corniche Mazraa, Said began to laugh so much that he stopped the car. 'Omar is at Galerie Semaan, waiting you. He brought some ammunition yesterday. They would not tell you because they did not trust you but they told me now because, I think, otherwise they would have laughed.'

'Oh Said, well done. Can we go there now? The military pressure is increasing and perhaps the ceasefire will go.'

Said looked doubtful. They could hear the occasional thump of heavy weapons from the south of the town. Since the incident at the port, Said had become most careful of his car.

'Drop me nearby,' Adam said quickly to forestall argument. 'It is safer for the car.'

South of the main road, the afternoon streets were quite empty. As they approached the slalom of red earthworks before the Galerie Semaan crossing, they could see that neither cars nor pedestrians were being allowed either way. The silence in the broad street was complete; and yet Adam had the queer impression that the area had only just been vacated. Rags hung limply from washing-lines on the broken balconies and the geraniums seemed to be prospering in their tins of milk-powder. Said turned into a blasted shop and turned off the engine.

'I will go with you,' he said without conviction.

'No,' said Adam. 'Stay here with the car. We must leave before dark. Wait for one hour and then call for me.'

Outside in the street, Adam had his old sensation of walking over broken glass. He shouted out that he was coming forward but something rushed over his head. He lay down amid the broken glass which did not cut him.

'Mister Adam. Mister Adam.' The voice was some distance away, at the end of the slalom.

'Yes. Can I come?'

'No. No. No. No,' the boy shouted but Adam was already stepping quickly along the burst pavement, his long shadow preceding him. Then he stopped and perched on one leg, teetering, for before him, scattered amid the little pieces of rubble and the broken glass, were cluster mines, their little black wings trembling in the almost horizontal sunlight. Adam turned round and they were, somehow, behind him too.

Adam began to shake but Omar appeared suddenly behind the nearest earthwork and reached across and pulled him over, hoisting him up with a rough jerk to stop his foot touching the ground.

'Why don't you clear those things away? They will cut off your leg if you tread on one.' Adam was angry. Another shell came overhead and they fell down onto the red earth.

'Do not be worried. They are firing mostly into the sea from Baabda. Not Galerie Semaan. Nobody comes here now.' He smiled in his way and picked up a stone. He put his foot on Adam's shoulder and slung the stone over the revetment, tumbling back in laughter as the blast blew over them.

'I, too, am a demolition expert,' he said and smiled.

By the time they had tiptoed through to the last barricade, the shelling was dying away and the fighters were breaking their fast in the cemetery of a ruined church. They looked a raggle-taggle bunch: an Eritrean, two silent Kurds, Omar and half a dozen Palestinians. A tomb had been hit and a dry old corpse lay among the fig suckers, with two little slippered feet peering out from the linen winding-sheet.

'This is General Sharon,' said Omar, lunging at the corpse with his rifle.

'Please,' said Adam. 'Because of the shelling can we go inside?' Despite his youth, Omar seemed to be the sergeant of the group.

'Of course.' The Eritrean followed them with food into the basement of an abandoned police station.

'I thought you would come,' Omar said, forcing food on Adam although it was not Adam who had fasted that long hot day. 'I doubted but then I thought you were a good man and would come.'

'Omar, I have a purpose.'

'You know I cannot answer questions on the military situation. There is our officer from Fatah but he is not here.'

'No, Omar. I am looking for one person.' Omar leaned back and drank deeply from a stone jug, smoothed down his uniform and took out an unopened packet of cigarettes.

'Is he a fighter?' The shelling now seemed to have stopped.

'I don't know. He is English.'

Omar suddenly stood up. 'Come. You must leave before it becomes too dark. Your comrade is with the fighters in the garden.' Adam's heart leapt and then he almost swooned with shame at forgetting Said among the cluster.

Adam took out his cigarette lighter and lit their way up the stairs.

'Omar,' he said to the boy's narrow back. 'Have you got a family?' The back stiffened a little in the flickering flame but there was no answer.

'This boy I'm looking for; he has a family in England.' Adam could feel cool air down the stairwell.

There was no answer. They reached the cemetery where Said had a rapt audience. He stood up furiously at the sight of Adam. Omar led them back through side streets, cupping a small torch.

'You will come tomorrow,' said Omar, shaking their hands.

'If the cease-fire continues,' Adam said hurriedly and got into the car.

For once Said drove slowly. They kept the lights off. As

they approached checkpoints, Said would stop and Adam shout out who they were. The streets were completely dark as if nobody lived in them any more.

'I'm sorry, Said. I thought you would wait just that little time.'

'Too much cluster,' said the boy crossly.

They did go back the next day, and the day after that, and Said even bundled Sharon, crackling, back into his ruined house out of deference to Adam's Christian feelings. Adam spent some time with the officer, who had been at Sandhurst before quitting the Jordanian Army; he had been wounded three times and even Said shut up in his presence.

The shelling had stopped altogether and old men and women with bundles were drifting back down the road to Chiyah, which Omar had now had cleared.

'They are somewhat rash,' said the officer.

'What do you think?' asked Adam.

'What do you think?' Smiling, he took Adam to the last barricade. Omar perched above him with his grenade launcher as he peered through a viewing window with a pair of beautiful East German fieldglasses.

A mile away, beside the furniture shop which had given its name to the crossing, a tank was being moved up, churning up the tarmac. Above, as Omar pointed him up the hill, Adam could make out two artillery pieces already dug in and camouflaged. Armoured personnel carriers were parked at the Baabda roundabout. Adam stepped down.

'Patience is not their virtue,' said the officer smartly, taking back his fieldglasses. 'A hot weekend. Heavy military pressure. Targets of opportunity. One cannot rule out a full assault.'

'But the Sabbath begins at sundown today.'

'Well, for us it's the Ramadan fast.' The officer laughed kindlily. 'You should be all right among the valiant warriors of Ras Beirut. Come back and see us when it's over, if we're still here.'

He put his hand firmly on Adam's chest and spun him round. Omar was standing quietly with his RPG. 'You are meeting this boy here at 0700 tomorrow. You will bring him back by 0800 or I'll have your guts for garters.'

125

Adam looked at Omar. He felt a sudden weariness.

'I have found your brother in Rouche. I wait you here early.'

Adam could not sleep. It was quite still but he kept turning over in his mind the meeting set for the morrow and, at about one o'clock when the local cockerels began their imbecile calling, he started thinking of Toby. Adam drew on his trousers and went downstairs.

The bar was empty but for Smith who sat, tightly in his soldierly way, before a large glass of orange juice.

'Hello, William.'

'Ah yes,' said Smith, swivelling his chair. His eyes were half-closed. 'I wanted to have a word with you. You had better get a drink. I am afraid it is self-service now but even old Etonians can occasionally serve themselves.'

Adam walked round the bar and found a tin of beer.

'You can have whisky, if you want,' said Smith. 'I don't object to you having whisky, if that is what you want.'

'I'd better lay off. It makes me frightened in the morning.' Adam reached over and picked out the vodka bottle, poured a lot into Smith's glass, and took a long swallow himself.

'You're right. I've been in an unholy funk all day. Must be drink.'

They sat in silence for a while. Adam wanted to tell Smith what he had seen above Galerie Semaan but thought better of it. Smith rested his head on his arms.

'You would know,' he said, squinting up at Adam. 'It's the moral cowards, the boozers, the womanisers, drug-takers too, I suppose, who crack first and let people down.' He closed his eyes. The dogs had started up now.

'Oh William, I'm frightened all the time and sometimes very frightened. So what.' Adam walked round the bar and brought back the vodka.

'Look at the nurses.' Smith did not appear to have been listening. 'They go down in the middle of the bombard-ment and do the most serious cases. We complain about getting shot at all for half-an-inch in the summary but here we are in the bar. We're the red-faced majors at the base.' He looked up at Adam in triumph.

'You remember that incident on the Green Line last year?'

'I have quite lost touch with the various disgraceful incidents people of your sort get involved in.' He put his head back down on his arms.

'You know the story. On the east side. Abandonment of comrades. Automatic fire and RPGs. Open ground. About 150 yards. Cover was overturned bus. Went first. Did not stop running. Did look back. Last member of party hit. Died.'

Smith was sitting bolt upright. 'Who was he?'

'You know perfectly well, William. It was Lukomski.'

'Who?' Smith had put his head down again. 'Don't know the name. Never really felt at home on that side. Was he with the Phalangists?'

Adam thought for a moment. 'He was East Beirut. More one can't say.'

'One can't say,' said Smith, imitating Adam's voice. 'Not too bad.'

'I still worry about it a lot.'

Smith got up smoothly. 'You can have some whisky if you need it.'

'Did you ever run Johnny's dog?'

Smith looked at him closely. 'You'd better have some,' he said. He strode steadily through the door.

CHAPTER TEN

Adam breakfasted alone at six o'clock. His vigil had made him hungry but when he asked the little Palestinian waitress for a boiled egg, she burst into tears and ran from the room. Adam followed her into the filthy kitchen. A single white egg sat in a dish by the sink.

'Look, Jauhara. Don't worry. I don't really like eggs. You keep that one for Mr Boutros.'

She continued to sob with her back to him. Adam put his arm round her.

'What's the matter? Is it your family? You know William will visit them when he goes to Sidon.' She shook her head vehemently and turned round.

'What will happen? How will it end? You must know. You and the other journalists.' She dried her eyes with a rag.

'Don't worry.' Adam tried to summon some confidence but he could not find it. 'They won't come into the city. The Americans won't let them. You'll be all right with us here.' He patted her on the head; but he had lost his appetite.

Outside Adam walked up and down but could not find Said. He hired the only driver around, an old fellow with pebble spectacles and a dripping nose who was, as Smith would have said, rear-echelon material. Adam was livid with Said.

Adam's anger only increased when the old man took the longest route conceivable to Galerie Semaan and when he found that Omar was not there. He cursed even poor little Jauhara.

The atmosphere was bad. In the side streets, armoured vehicles or trucks mounted with recoilless rifles were parked, and young men were hurrying about in pairs. He kept showing Hassan's pass, now a week out of date, but nobody had heard of Omar. At last, he found the Eritrean, sitting quite still in the cemetery, who told him in weird Italian that the situation was bad, the unit had moved and Omar was sorry but he must go to Rouche alone.

'But Rouche's a big place.' All those tall apartment blocks; he could be in any one of them. 'Where is the unit? Where is Omar?'

The Eritrean looked nervous. 'Borj al-Brajnie. Point Six. Go.'

Oh my God, thought Adam, of all places.

The driver had contrived to get lost. Adam plunged into a burned-out shop and started shouting for him.

'O driver,' he cried softly, for he did not even know the old man's name. 'O driver,' he cried again. Something heavy and slow was moving in the street behind him; more steady than a tank, and anyway these creeps had so few, too big for a bulldozer; some sort of heavy gun, perhaps, or a Katyusha rocket launcher, who cared; Adam had to leave before these boys become tired of waiting and started it all.

The old man creaked up in his hopeless car. 'You fool,' said Adam. 'Let's go, quickly.' The old fellow lurched off.

'Benzine,' he said wheezily, wiping his nose on his sleeve and slowing back down to a crawl.

'You silly old fool. There's no benzine here. Go to Borj al-Brajnie, now, at once, as fast as you can, slowing down only at checkpoints.'

The driver stared at Adam through his pebble glasses and stopped the car. 'No. Too much danger. Go Admiral.'

'Do as I say.' Adam shouted at him and pushed the lever into gear so that they bounded forward.

Borj al-Brajnie was quite empty. The little concrete hovels down the camp streets seemed uninhabited. The few poor shops were closed.

'Stop here.' A uniformed scarecrow pointed a twisted anti-aircraft gun at the sky in a gesture of pathetic defiance. Before the sand-bagged entrance to a basement was a map of mandate Palestine and the Arabic numeral 6, done up in red, black and white pebbles.

'Drop you here. I wait you at the Admiral.'

'No you don't.' Adam tore the keys out of the ignition and ran down the stairs of the command post. At the bottom, he collided into Omar.

'My dear, why have you come?' He smiled with great sweetness.

'I must know where in Rouche. Please, it will begin soon.'

Omar smiled again. 'Come inside and drink coffee and take your rest.'

'Are you mad, Omar?'

'I think you are frightened.'

'I am. Please, Omar. He is my brother.'

'The new building opposite Sud Engineering. You can go now.' He turned away but Adam had gone.

The old man shot off in his car. 'You are like a mad. I tell Mr Boutros.'

'It doesn't matter now. Go.' They had reached the straight boulevard between Chatila and the Forêt des Pins. This is where they come down, following the road, so low you can see the markings under the wings, then they go up almost vertically in a great flash, with the flak bursting out of Chatila cemetery. Please, no aircraft, please; and then Adam heard the first explosion on his left.

'Go Admiral,' whispered the driver and plunged forward down the empty Boulevard. A Fatah Range-Rover screamed out of a side-street, its back and sides plastered with red mud, but the old man just thundered past it, turning into Fakhani as the uniformed driver lazily raised his rifle to fire over them.

'Don't overtake military vehicles, you imbecile.' Adam was beside himself with rage and fear. 'Go Rouche. Now. Leave me there.'

The shells were coming in fast, with no more than a second between them, ahead of the car and to their left. Adam craned his neck but could see nothing above his head. They turned off Corniche Mazraa and turning, Adam saw, far out to sea, a flash of white fire. He twiddled the knob of the radio which came off in his hand.

'Get me Kataib radio. Quickly.'

'Not work,' said the driver.

'You half-wit.'

Adam got rid of the old man and rested beside a roast-chicken shop at the highest point in Rouche. There was nobody to be seen. Adam shaded his eyes to try and find the gunboat but he could see only bursts of white smoke along the sea-road to the airport. A haze hung over the hills but there were flashes of fire there, too, among the Aleppo pines and great mushrooms of red and yellow smoke where the shells were falling on his left. If they stick south of Corniche Mazraa, Adam thought, and if there are no aircraft, I could . . .

'Can I give assistance?'

Adam got up sheepishly. A young fighter was standing before him, trailing his rifle and holding out a red hibiscus.

'Hello,' said Adam. 'I am a journalist and looking for my friend who is an officer here in Rouche, I think with Fatah. I want to see him to explain certain military aspects of the attack so I can write it for my newspaper. I think he must be here at a position in a high building.' Adam took the proffered flower.

'I think you are English,' said the young man, running back to a hibiscus bush on the waste ground behind him and taking a bloom for himself. 'Welcome.'

They set off down across a piece of waste ground between two rows of tall blocks of flats. In fact, Adam noticed, the waste ground with its hibiscus and wild figs was an abandoned construction site which stretched all the way down to the sea front. The southernmost of the apartment buildings on their left hand, and the nearest to the sea, was marked Sud Engineering. As they descended, Adam glimpsed clouds of smoke between the buildings on their left.

The boy took him into the newest of the blocks on the right. The staircase banister trembled a little with the distant explosions. Adam counted to the fifth floor and saw, through the window, the ferris wheel of the shuttered Lunapark.

On the landing, the boy made a great noise of scuffling feet and rifle-dragging, and then they entered on a small room full of women. 'Bring coffee,' he said. The women shrank back, smiling: then the boy lost his poise and Adam walked ahead of him into the large drawing room.

It was spotlessly clean. The windows had been slid back and the curtains attached round them with twine. The heavy fake Louis XV sofas had not been sat in; a pile of magazines rested undisturbed on a side-table, beside an unopened box of Davidoff cigars and a bottle of Otard. At one window, an old man stood in his vest on a sheet of polythene covering a Nain carpet, his shoes off, watering some plants. At the other, the window facing south, a young man in uniform and with brilliant red hair was looking intently through field glasses attached to a tripod. He carried no revolver but a radio swung at his belt.

Adam walked towards the young man, his steps leaving deep marks in a rich white carpet that reminded him of Toby's house in Ireland.

The young man continued looking through his field glasses, then spoke quickly in Arabic into his radio. He straightened and turned round and with one sweep of his eyes cleared out the old man and the boy. Unlike the teenaged fighters Adam had met, the young man's uniform made him seem younger not older, but his face was thin and his blue eyes so weary that Adam thought for a moment of poor blind Laura. He had not shaved.

'Hello, Adam,' he said, smiling like a Palestinian. 'Hot day, I'm afraid.' Johnny Penrose turned back to his tripod. His shoulders twitched a little. Adam stared at the back for a while.

'Do you want me to come back when you've finished your work?' Nothing and nobody stays still, Adam thought; everybody moving about like little balls on a flat surface, he thought.

'The Palestine Revolution has never finished its work,' Johnny said and turned round with a smile. 'As you are here, you might as well stay and watch south Beirut burn. The ladies will bring coffee.' He called out gently to them.

Adam dropped into the sofa with his back to the window. He could hear the explosions behind him but he did not wish to see them. Once in the deep sofa, he reached out for something. 'Would it be looting to have some of this delicious brandy?'

'Yes, it would.' Johnny did not look up but stepped back from the window and sat on the sofa back. 'Adam, you don't have to act a part any more.'

'Don't blame the boy, Johnny,' Adam said quickly. 'I've been looking for you for two weeks. You've made an impression. I was lucky or you kept your word. There was someone at the Museum.'

'Of course. Of course.' He looked more warmly at Adam. 'I could never keep a secret. Just like Toby. How is he?'

'Dead. In a motor accident.'

Johnny's face creased for a moment and then he regained himself. 'I'm sorry. And Laura? How has she taken it?'

'She went a bit wonky. But they say she'll be all right. She's in Scotland.'

'He should have come here, you know. Can't you understand?' He seemed about to explain and then lost interest and stood up briskly, taking Adam's upper arm. 'So. What can I do for you?' He took Adam out onto the open balcony.

'They are hitting their largest area yet, a big arc or semicircle from the Airport and Borj al-Brajnie in the south right up to Sabra and Chatila and Corniche Mazraa. As far as I can see, they are not coming north of that.' He bent down to his field glasses. 'I understand they are pushing up armour beside the airport but they are not committing their air force for reasons you can guess as well or better than I.' He looked up at Adam. 'You always grind your teeth. I'm not sure there are any dentists left.'

'I'm sorry.' Adam put his hand to his mouth.

'Immediately in front of you is a building called Sud Engineering. Between that and the next building on the landward side, you can see a cloud of fire and ochre smoke. This is a phosphorus shell, probably fired from the Chouf about 25 miles away to the south. Later on, the boy will take you to AUH to show you the effect of phosphorus.' He looked up and smiled gently. 'Even when they are dead, the children go on burning inside for hours. Pinch their noses and see.'

'Stop it,' said Adam.

Johnny swivelled the field glasses to the right. 'The large building on the sea-shore is the Summerland Hotel. That is taking fire from our friend out to sea and from a rocket position near or at the Khalde crossroads about 9 miles away. Our rockets, originally, by the way. They seem to think there is a terrorist emplacement in the two underground garages below the hotel.'

Adam peered through the glasses. The hotel was burning black and fiercely.

'Is there?'

'No comment.'

'Oh, Johnny, I did not trail you all over Beirut for this.' Bubbles of air seemed to have found their way into his chest. 'Are you coming with me?'

'Aha. So you are Sir Donald's one-man peace mission?' He laughed unconvincingly.

'No. I mean yes, I saw your father but that was before it all . . .'

'There they go.' Johnny straightened and pointed to the shore deep to the south. Adam thought he could make out an even line of puffs of smoke.

'One, two, three, four, five,' Johnny counted but Adam could now see the rockets themselves, coming in at their level and then dipping suddenly, their tails all fire. He was crouched down and saw, through the balcony railings, the rockets seem to step across the water in bursts of red fire and black smoke until they reached the Summerland. It seemed to last for ever for before the last had burst, the sound of the first had reached them.

'All the tubes. All 40.' Johnny spoke again into his radio.

'It's nothing to do with your father or Laura, though, God knows, she needs you. It's the others. They are worried you might be captured.'

'Not killed? They needn't be, you know, Adam. Poor Adam, how did they get hold of you?'

Adam's chest felt like bursting. He could see himself walking across at the Museum, alone, alive, tired but whole; Mary, Laura, Scotland. He fumbled with his cigarettes.

'Listen,' said Johnny. Adam listened. Above the rumbling from the south, he heard something slow and heavy, just as he had that morning down by Galerie Semaan, although the roads were better here.

'We can't let them have it all their own way . . .'

'But Johnny, what happens if Arafat does take you all out? I don't care about the, I mean the people in London, but if the Israelis find you, an Englishman, either here or on the way out, they'll hold you. That's what they're worried about.'

The heavy, slow sound stopped. Adam walked quickly to the end of the balcony. It was a multiple rocket launcher and had reversed onto the waste ground. The driver had opened his door on the far side and must have stepped down; another man was making the front wheels firm; two others were doing something to the banks of tubes. Their faces were almost black and they worked quickly and with concentration. Adam thought of the demons in a Bosch Inferno. At the top of the hill, some lunatic was tinkering with the engine of his car.

The men jumped back, holding their ears and tumbling on the ground amid the fig suckers. The rockets went off in a white flash and a great hot blast that filled Adam's shirt. Johnny peered once into his field glasses, then spoke into the radio.

'Well, Adam, I am sorry to say the Palestine Revolution is firing into the sea.' He stood before Adam with his hands on his hips. His eyes had become friendly and compassionate.

'Look, Johnny. You know I'm right. For God's sake. What happens if this lot find out? About you? About me?'

'I think you knew Hussein Sarabi, didn't you?' Johnny Penrose sighed. 'The funny thing is that this town is crawling with Israeli agents and they had to pick him, the best man they had.'

'Oh my God.' Adam reached out and fidgeted with the twine binding the curtains to the big sheets of unbroken window. 'Come with me. It's not worth it, is it? You don't need a passport. We'll bring you over through Sodeco, Said knows the place, my driver, and he knows the local armed elements who have a business arrangement with the Kataib.

Someone will meet us the other side and fix Schlomo.' He stood up straight and tried to look Johnny clearly in the eyes but there was something new in them, more than friendliness; anxiety, perhaps.

'Poor old Adam. You, of all people, should know that accidents happen in Sodeco.'

'That was an accident.'

'Perhaps. But isn't it strange that of those who knew of Butterworth's grand strategy and the deal that was worked out, Lukomski is dead, Hussein is under arrest and I wouldn't give old Bachir long after this is over. That leaves me, and Butterworth. And now you, poor fellow. The thing is, Adam, they wanted war and nobody was going to stop them.'

Then Adam woke up as if he had been sleep-walking and saw in Johnny's eyes the depths of his own foolishness and knew that for days, months, years he had got the world slightly wrong, as if he carried a watch that lost a few minutes, and in this sudden understanding he heard again the sound of something heavy and slow.

'Oh God, Johnny. You're mad. Barking mad. This is nothing to do with me. You called that thing up. How long have we got? How long?'

'Well, they're rather quick and they can use the Khalde position. Let's say, a minute to identify, two or three minutes to transmit, two minutes to adjust and load up, if they aren't already. Let's say three minutes from now.'

Adam began to walk quickly across the carpet, leaving deep marks beside his earlier prints. The young Lebanese peered round the door and behind him, Adam saw the women filing down the staircase. Johnny detached his field glasses and snapped the tripod shut.

'Why don't you stay?' he said quietly. 'You've got nothing better and they won't leave you alone. Your Arabic is okay and I'll be here. We ought to stick together, in a way. With Toby gone.'

There was no appeal in his voice. As he ushered Adam through the door, he half-closed his eyes. Adam felt an overwhelming urge to say yes, not to worry about getting out, about Mary and Scotland, but to get through this bit and then, after that, to do his thinking.

Johnny held open the door onto the landing. 'Almost there,' he said and then the boy sprang in, saying, 'Now, now, Captain John,' and they were running down the marble stairs, fourth floor, the steel rail still firm to the touch, third floor, second floor, and then the rail trembled. 'Move,' Johnny shouted, almost picking him up, but Adam had seen something, down below, through the entrance hall, a red car with a deep gash down its beautiful paintwork and its driver staring wildly through the open door, and Adam jumped over the rail and shouted goodbye, and he was falling, like Toby, falling, like Lukomski, falling onto broken glass.

'You're finished,' Johnny shouted and the glass was jumping from the floor but Adam was up and running and the car was moving and as he landed in the back, it seemed to take off, all four wheels, and then to fall back and burst up the hill like a bullet. Then the windows starred and Said's wild face was bleeding and Adam's mouth was full of red earth. Adam could see through his open door and the rockets were slapping into Johnny's building, second floor, then in great bursts of black smoke and red flame into the floors above. The balcony at the top began to tumble down, window frames and furniture and the old man's pot plants, slipping down as if in a broken doll's house. A last rocket drove in without exploding.

Said stopped the car just over the brow of the hill, beside the roasted chicken shop. He was crying. Adam fell out into the road and crawled under the forward door which was all twisted. There was blood on Said's face and shirt. Adam put his arm through and hugged him round the waist. He felt the muscle in the boy's stomach.'

'Alive, Said?'

'Thanks be to God.' Tears streaked his dirty face and greasy drops of blood fell down onto his shirt, which Adam had never seen changed. There was no injury to the chest.

'So you came.'

'Of course. The old man told me you were in Rouche. I went only for benzine. Why, why, why?' He wiped his face with tissues from a box on the dashboard and adjusted himself in the mirror.

Adam sat down on the edge of the door. 'So, best of all friends, there is bad damage to the car, which is my responsibility. You must see how it is with the car.'

Adam raised himself up. His legs were trembling and he was bleeding from the old bandage on his elbow. His eyes stung with grit. 'I must go down and see if they are all right.'

Said sprang out of the car and pulled Adam's shirt front so tight that it tore. The rip bit into his throat. 'No, you don't,' he whispered close into Adam's ear. 'They just want you for themselves. Who was it who came for you among the bombs?' Adam struggled. He had not seen eyes so mad. 'Who was it who drove down after the Katusha to find you? They just want to keep you there and then *suwarikh* come again, after five minutes, after ten hours.' He let Adam go and stared at the ground in shame.

'Poor Said,' Adam said. Smoke was billowing from the upper stories. Adam shielded his eyes but could see nothing along the shoreline to the south. They began to run. In the hall, Adam tripped and fell. Bursts of heat were rolling down the stairs and the stair rail had come loose. The steel door to the basement was fast.

'Johnny!' he whispered, then shouted. 'Johnny!'

'Now. The boat! The boat!' Said was dancing in the road.

Adam tripped again and, falling, saw the red earth burst in the centre of the waste ground. Said was on his face. Adam got up and ran.

'We will go,' said Adam, when they reached the car again. 'First to the American Hospital for your face and then to that place where you took the car before. Maybe, if you agree, we will paint it another colour.' He closed the back door roughly and it came free in his hand.

They did not go at once to the hospital. Turning into Rue Bliss, Said turned the car into an underground garage and jumped out. Adam got out, too, still holding the door and tested his legs. He leaned himself and the door against the car and listened to the explosions walking about behind him, along the Rouche seafront, the other side of the peninsula. The garage smelt of grease and humans.

As his eyes became accustomed to the darkness, Adam saw that he was not alone. Along all three walls were rows of eyes, watching him shyly. The eyes belonged to women bound up in rags and coloured cloth and children struggling in their arms. At the end of the room a baby started to cry.

'Hello,' said Adam.

There was a clamour of female greeting and heavy moving about as each one made a place for him to sit amid the bolsters and bedding, cooking pots, flashlights, stoves, cheap suitcases, babies. They began to whisper among themselves and, gradually, the children broke free and skipped towards him.

Adam braced his legs and picked up the first two, little girls in torn party frocks and white socks, with dirty faces and tangled hair. Adam leaned back against the car to support their weight.

As they nuzzled into his neck and struggled to find a comfortable position, Adam felt acutely the strength and pliancy of their limbs.

Said emerged softly beside them, whisked up the two girls and put them in the car. Beside him were two silent mechanics who began to examine the bodywork with flashlights. Said ran his hand down the deep gash, which the rocket launcher must have made when it passed.

The first little girl still held onto Adam's hand, sitting quietly in the back seat, but the car was now filling up. Adam could not believe there could be so many children, running in from their homes by the walls and diving into the car. The front was a living mass of shrieking children.

'I'll pay for the repairs, Said. It is my responsibility. Let us paint it green, the colour of paradise. I will pay!'

Said was showing the mechanics the damaged doors and the starred windows. 'No. It is for me. You little Satan!' He reached in and extracted a little boy who had found the horn; but another immediately took his place, and then a third, and the long wail of the horn drowned the sound of walking about on the other side of the peninsula.

'Fucking Katusha,' Said said and bent to discuss money with the mechanics.'

'Language, Said! Anyway, it's Katyusha. The Russians always call their weapons after girls.'

The mechanics brought up a gas mantle lamp and started ejecting the children. Said and Adam walked away but the first little girl followed them up the ramp. Adam saw her, not quite daring to cross the bar of shadow into the sunlight. He returned and gave her a five-lire note.

They walked to the hospital but did not go in. Two Volkswagen ambulances had collided in the courtyard and armed men were screaming and firing above their heads. Perhaps it was their families being handed out of the ambulances.

Said touched his face. 'It is not important,' he said, but a nurse with very long black hair broke away from the ambulance door and approached them. Her wrist was bandaged.

'*Sind Sie verletzt?*' She looked Adam up and down.

'*Nein, Gott sei dank. Mein Freund aber . . . was sollen wir mit seinem Gesicht tun?*' She returned to the ambulance and brought a spray of water and a bottle of something. Her eyes were almost black.

Said sat down on a low wall as she began to clean his face.

'We were in Rouche at the start of the bombardment,' Adam said quickly to her white-coated back. The German came very strangely to him. 'An apartment block was hit directly by rockets. There were people inside . . .'

'Yes. Right opposite Sud Engineering. There were women. Shock and one sprain, only. *Gott sei dank.*' She stood up, patted Said on the shoulder and gave him some instructions. Her shoulders, too, Adam noticed, drooped with tiredness.

Adam stood in her way. 'Where did you learn your German?'

'Excuse me.' She tried to pass him. 'We are all busy. In Leipzig, Karl Marx Uniklinik.' She smiled and Adam let her pass.

He watched her walk back towards the ambulance, her

white coat spreading out behind her. Said put his arm through Adam's and led him away.

'She is too much busy.' His face was a mass of yellow blotches. 'Katieusha,' he said and slapped Adam on the back. 'You want a beer?'

They had turned down towards the university. 'Not yet, Said. Let's go and sit in the university garden and take our rest.'

They sat on a bench under the *pins maritimes*, or rather Adam sat for Said immediately sprang up and disappeared. Adam supposed he had gone for the beer and was going to make a speech.

The bombardment seemed a long way away in Rouche, the other side of the peninsula. Boys sat reading on the benches against the stone New England buildings or played chess under the trees. A little apart, the girls sat, talking quietly to one another or watching the games. Some wore white linen tabards, stamped Civil Defence in Arabic, and a red cross had been painted on the ground. They shook their hair about and turned away when they saw Adam watching them, and then stared back and smiled almost imperceptibly. Adam wanted to touch them.

'Will you marry?' asked Said, following Adam's stare. He handed him a cold beer wrapped in tissue paper.

'I hope so.' Adam tried to conjure Mary but she seemed too pale. 'I want to marry Katyusha.'

Said looked shocked. 'She is beautiful, of course,' he said doubtfully. 'But she is Palestinian.'

'She would become English if she married me.'

'She will always be Palestinian, even in England. And,' he said, laughing, 'she has brothers who will come and make difficulties for you if you treated her badly.' Adam thought of the gentle Ferdinand.

'Said, I don't think we should speak about girls. It only makes us uncomfortable. Especially after a great danger.'

'You are right.' He reached into a bag for another beer.

'I think she loves you. She spoke with you in the German language.'

'That's enough.'

They sat in silence for some time, listening to the bombardment and the rush of wind through the *pins maritimes*. Snatches of conversation floated by from the chess-players or the girls, but mostly they sat quietly, moving the pieces, or hugging their knees. Occasionally, a loudspeaker would call one of the tabarded girls to duty.

'They had a big gun here, before, at the beginning of the war.' Said pointed down the steep garden past the heavy stone buildings. Could this be the speech, Adam wondered.

'Yes. I heard. On the tennis courts.'

'They said they had to put the gun here to protect these streets against the boats. But the professors said, "No, if you put the gun here, they will shoot at us and the university will be burned." And the captain said: "This is our responsibility. We must defend these quarters." And the professors said, "Look, the hospital will be hit also." And so they took away the gun and put it by the sea where it was destroyed.'

'Yes. I heard. Just like the rockets in Rouche. Next they will come to Hamra.'

Said stared at him cleverly. 'I think I know why you went to that place. Every day, first the Museum, then Sodeco, then Galerie Semaan, then Borj al-Brajnie, the old man said, and at last Rouche.' He smiled with pride. 'You were looking for one man, even when you were going to Reuter. I think it was John. And now, you want me to change the colour of my car, because you think, maybe, one man is looking for you.'

'Maybe,' said Adam. Then Adam began to make his speech. 'You remember, last year, when you picked me up from the Kataib in Karantina and we had to do the crossing at night.'

Said nodded and made a great show of shivering at the memory. The girls were looking at them. Adam went on more softly: 'You remember I wept. I wept because I thought I had not been brave.' Adam looked round at the golden buildings, the pines, the chess-players and the girls, the red cross on the tarmac. He breathed out a great sigh of pleasure. 'I ran away when the Liberation Army shot at us but it does not matter. It is a matter of knowing what you are and where you belong. I am weak, I know that.'

'Don't say that to Katieusha.' Said laughed.

'That's enough.' They got up and walked slowly towards the gate.

'We're leaving,' Smith said firmly, and pushed past Adam to the lift. 'Pack your things, settle your bill. I'll explain later.' The generator had been turned off and the lift was not working. Smith was forced to turn for the stairs, avoiding Adam's eye, lest he lose his air of firm but indefinable purpose.

The atmosphere in the Admiral was queer. The front desk staff was bent down to its work and no one looked up as Adam wandered back towards the door. A large branch appeared through the door of the bar, and then two tiny Goanese servants under it. They seemed unsure what to do with their burden. The cashier shouted at them crossly.

Boutros was slumped in his green chair.

'What's up?' asked Adam, sitting down beside him.

'Your arm is bleeding again. This is a hotel, not a bloody first aid post. Get it seen to.' Then he relented.

'I've had enough of those goons, pissing about here in their Newsweek shirts as if they own the place. They're out, I tell you. I don't pay anybody; not Palestinians, sodding Murabitoun, not Kataib, nobody. You all complain about the hotel. No eggs today. Losing all the laundry. But I've kept it open for you for seven bloody years. You think I make money out of this joint?' He looked at Adam accusingly, waving at the sleaziness around him and the frightened Goanese.

'My main operation is in London now. You know why I keep this clip joint going?'

Adam stood up. 'Pride, I suppose, Boutros. But you wouldn't keep it going if it lost you money.'

'Bloody right I wouldn't. I'm a businessman, not a wet-nurse for journalists. And get that arm seen to.' He strode off to his office.

Something seemed to have gone wrong on the security front. Adam wandered outside, looking for the captain of the guard and the warriors, but they had vanished from their usual station by the door. Adam found them 50 yards up the street, seated in a row before an open grocery. They had taken their chairs with them, or perhaps these were part of their equipment, like the AK-47 rifles or the tee-shirts.

'Welcome,' said Adam. The captain budged up, forcing the most junior to vacate his seat at the end and, in compensation, moodily to examine his weapon as if this had always been his intention.

'It was purely my decision,' said the captain softly. 'Based on the military situation on the ground. An exchange of fire in the lobby would have been disastrous. It was therefore my responsibility to retire to the basement to be in a position to launch an attack at a more favourable moment. Like Rommel, the rat of the desert.'

Adam coughed. 'I am sure you were right. Anybody hurt?'

'Thanks be to God.' The captain touched his heart.

'Who was it?'

'Nasserites. Two groups. On the one hand, Murabitoun, on the other hand, Shaab al-Amal. That apartment.' He nodded towards the block of flats abutting the hotel. It was pitted with bullet marks and had jagged holes for windows. A little smoke was still drifting out. Adam could now see the hotel trees had been decapitated.

'They were moving people from Rouche. For safety. On the one hand, Duschka recoilless, on the other hand, RPG. It was a foolish battle,' said the captain sanctimoniously and then, in a softer tone: 'Do you know Mr Boutros?'

'Of course,' said Adam, getting up and coughing once more. 'Please don't worry. I will speak to him.'

He went to Smith's room, stopping only at the front desk in case they had started making up the bills. They had not. Smith was packing.

'So what if they ran away,' Adam said immediately. 'I would have done. Those Duschkas go through walls.'

Smith waved impatiently. 'That is not the point. These people think they have a monopoly of violence. Well, I'm afraid, in my case, at least, that is not true. I was a soldier. That water-skier pointed the Duschka at us and fired at the hotel when we tried to stop him. We're moving out of this area, until I've considered the best response.'

'Why should I? I'm safer here. Did Butterworth tell you to say that? William. Answer me.'

'What? Who?' Smith looked up from his suitcase. He seemed shocked by Adam's tone.

'I'm sorry, William. We got stuck in the bombardment of Rouche. It rather takes it out of one. Have you done your story for Sunday?'

Smith nodded.

'Well, let's have a drink and I'll tell you about the beautiful Kate.'

'There is no monopoly of violence,' said Smith, darkly, but he came down to the bar.

CHAPTER ELEVEN

A ceasefire came into force at midnight. Sunday was quiet but for the rattle of gunfire from the south as the Palestinians buried their dead. By the afternoon, hordes of people were returning on foot from the eastern side to check their homes were intact or to pick through the rubble for their possessions.

The Palestinians were leaving at last! This immense message emerged more clearly from M. Le Président's florid French than from Hassan's crisp English.

Adam found the great man in his study, surrounded as ever by signed photographs of Arab kings and French intellectuals, although he had now renounced, with great sorrow, the famous rose in his lapel until the killing should stop. He was first and foremost and understandably anxious that something of his once beautiful city, which had done more than its share for the Palestinian cause, be spared. *Mais ce Sharon là-bas* . . .

Hassan, in contrast, had nowhere to go which was not, either geographically or psychologically, further from his Palestine. Adam suspected that Hassan had come to believe, as he sat by his telex machine through those black Fakhani nights, that each day he survived in the city improved his condition and that each car bomb, each shattered building, each child burned by phosphorus or damaged by cluster, was wounding his enemy as much as it wounded him; and that what Smith or Adam were writing, or the networks displaying on television, was causing hands to be wrung in London, Bonn, Paris and in Washington, the capital of the world. Might not something be salvaged, something remain in this lovely city to protect the poor and the weak from the vengeance of their enemies? Or might it not be, by some queer logic of war, that the Palestinians might lose the battle but achieve what years of equivocation and incompetent violence had failed to achieve: a name and a place at table?

Adam returned to Johnny's building in Rouche and though the civil defence workers warned him of an unexploded rocket, he tiptoed again into the ruined entrance hall. For a block of flats, and a block of flats in Beirut, it was well built. The basement was intact. Adam could find no trace of men and women except, in the light of a flaring match, a single hibiscus bloom.

Nunc dimittis. Walking back from Rouche, with the sea on his left hand and the Lunapark before him, he thought of Butterworth. ('Quite a good effort, I felt, although he proved too obstinate for you. Though I myself had no illusions about the security situation, we were, in general, perhaps somewhat sanguine. You had a certain degree of good fortune in meeting the boy at the Museum but you evaluated his remarks correctly, your only lead, incidentally, when Sarabi, as I had feared, came to grief. I would perhaps have liked a greater attention to cover . . .') Adam's immediate anxiety, as he walked towards Reuters, was Smith. Smith had vanished. Adam wondered if his friend's dark talk of a response, which he had returned to ever more often and obsessively as they had drunk through the evening, might not embrace some military action against the armed elements around the hotel.

Behind the perspex windows, he wrote a long eye-witnesser of the events of the previous day but without giving Johnny a name or a nationality. The Reuters boys had painstakingly compiled an estimate of the casualties admitted to the hospitals. With no Sunday edition, and the day of rest in Europe, the *DT* might use a sentence or two. The story came easily. It was as if the rattle of typewriter keys steadied his civilian nerves as the gunmen rattled off their weapons at the sky to steady theirs. Adam also composed a stern service message to the foreign editor, no less, complaining about the irregular playbacks, reminding of the absence of foreign newspapers and hinting of risk in Beirut and irresponsibility in London. He returned to the

Admiral and fell asleep, and thus missed what he would have otherwise attended, a press conference where Hassan displayed some men who had, he said, confessed to setting car bombs for the enemy.

The next morning, Said turned up in front of the hotel with what looked like a brand new, red Chevrolet. Adam stood in the road with his hands on his hips. Said was embarrassed and explained that the car, after all, was not entirely his own property; rather, it belonged to a syndicate of his father and uncles and the word drifting back from Achrafiyeh was that red was a perfectly suitable colour, especially in a bad security situation. Said's only concessions to Adam's new discretion was the pair of wrap-around, silvered sun glasses he wore and a similar pair resting on the dashboard for Adam.

Adam was exhausted. The Palestinians, who had survived another day, were setting new conditions for their departure. When Adam came to Point 11, the one about the Palestine Cinema Institute retaining its headquarters in Beirut, he gave up. Said, too, was behaving strangely as if he had some plan afoot. He was anxious to take Adam down to Sabra but would not reveal why.

Adam made one excursion, to Reuters, to pick up his playback, and then retired to the Admiral bar where Smith found him, drunk, at six o'clock.

'Ah. Can I read your service? I never get them.'

'Of course. Can I just tear off a personal bit at the top? I wouldn't want Boutros to hear how poor I am.' Adam folded the message in half on the table and clumsily tore off the answerback.

'Blast,' he said. 'I'm a bit plastered.' But he had the message off by heart.

promurray care reuter beirut exdeetee ldn 252300 pls onpass

regret yr eyewitnesser outsqueezed peso revaluation etc. much apc yr efforts so far but gtful deeper analysis of pal options when how where to query. ed most unimpressed colour and daredevilry but feels eastside move riskiest till above cleared. stg 100 rpt 1000 trsfd ac boutros wazzan, manny hanny, ldn, rgds desk

'Typical,' said Smith. 'Staff officers. I read your piece on the Reuters outgoing and it seemed all right to me.'

'Thank you, William. You are kind.' Smith was right. It was, in many ways, a typical *DT* service message. Yet Adam's eyewitnesser, unusually for a colour piece, and even more so for one from a stringer, had run outside, on that morning's back page, as a message from the foreign editor, no less, had told him before he burned it. The answerback Adam had clumsily torn off was not the absurd TRUTH G of Beacon House but EXRES G, which defined a machine that was the most substantial piece of furniture in a small office in Bruton Street. Adam put his head in his hands.

'Look. You've been at it rather. Why don't you slip out of the city for a day or two?'

Adam looked at Smith carefully. 'I'm going nowhere but Palestine.'

'That's what I mean. You're getting all wound up in the story. Go over to the other side. I was there on Sunday. You feel better in five minutes. Like breathing oxygen on a hangover. Go through the Museum . . .'

'So that's it, Smith, is it? You think I can't find him. You think you can do it, you bastard.'

'Adam, what's the matter with you?' Smith reached across and shook Adam's shoulder. 'Pull yourself together, Adam. You're playing into their hands. That's what a siege is for. To break down trust, to make us hate one another, so that they can come in quietly one morning.'

'I'm sorry, but . . .'

'I know it's hard for you, what with your friend dying and everything. Take a day out.'

'I'm sorry, William. But the *DT's* Tel Aviv man is doing the eastern side. Loves the Kataib. So disciplined, he says. Bachir not at all a thug. Did not kiss cook. Lebanon's hope. Probably right.'

'He is. All right. So you think you belong on this side. Why not take a trip to the south and see what Schlomo is up to down there. You could have another bash looking for Jauhara's father.'

Adam got up and brought more whisky from the bar. They went on drinking all evening, though Jauhara brought Smith an uneven steak and Adam some boiled rice where they sat. The bar became noisy and quarrelsome and then subsided. The barman came over and apologised: midnight had struck and they must serve themselves at the bar. The Reuters boys went off to write their daylead and returned and went to bed. The circle came down to four, Smith and Adam, and two American photographers in safari suits and bullet-proof vests.

'You've got to get close . . .'

'You can't cover this war in high heels . . .'

The two photographers said the same things but in different ways. They were Californian. Listening to them, Adam conjured lawns and swimming pools, tended by placid negroes, and immense motor cars throwing back the light. The whisky tasted like milk.

'You've got to get right in close . . .' Adam closed an eye and they merged into a single person. He wondered if it would go to bed.

'Like I said. You can't cover this war in high heels . . .'

'You're a fool.' Smith looked up at the repetition of this sentence. 'Look at the nurses. They go down in the middle of the bombardment, to the targets, to treat the worst cases.'

'I know a girl . . .' Adam stopped. The world had reduced to a small circle of light but he was not that drunk. Smith peered up at him with one eye.

'That's the real reason, isn't it? Your driver was saying. The girl at the hospital in Sabra, what's it called, Gaza.'

'If Said talked a bit less and drove a bit better, we'd all be much happier.' Still, Adam was pleased; but Gaza, wasn't that always being hit? How could they keep it going down there? Adam spun round in his chair and focussed on the door. 'Hey. You can't come in here. No guns allowed in here.' The boy stopped obediently at the entrance.

'Nonsense,' said Smith, swivelling round. 'There have always been guns round this bar,' he said mysteriously. He got up, walked steadily towards the boy and took the AK-47 from him. He snapped the magazine off and began to examine the weapon.

'After you with that . . .'

'Pass it over here . . .'

'For God's sake, William. There's one in the barrel. You don't need that thing. Put it down. Young man, what do you want?'

The boy walked shyly to the bar. 'Press conference,' he said.

'Are you mad? It's two in the morning.' Where was the captain of the guard? Why hadn't Boutros kept him on?

'Press conference. At the Phoenicia. The men have been tried.'

'Which men? The car bombers? The alleged car bombers?'

The boy nodded. 'And one other man, who was their leader.'

'I think I'll give this one a miss,' said Adam.

Smith, who was squinting down the barrel, nodded.

'What's up with Britain . . .'

'Lost its bottle, has it . . .'

Smith raised the rifle slowly. 'Never, never, let your gun, pointed be at any one.' He lowered the barrel, stood up and handed rifle and magazine to the boy.

'Fucking British loony . . .'

'Arsehole . . .'

They got into the back of the boy's jeep. 'I was there when Hassan put them on show,' Smith said quietly. 'Some of the dear colleagues were of the view that since they had been displayed to *Time* and *Newsweek* and the networks, they might merely be disciplined.' He laughed. 'One said his family had been held by Kataib gunmen unless he drove the car in and another something about hashish.'

'Not hashish,' Adam said.

'Yes, the other stuff. Heroin. He said an Israeli officer had produced some heroin. He said he needed it. That was the one by the Prime Minister's place that almost had your number.'

'Did you believe them?'

'Oh, who knows? A bit crude for the Israelis, I would have thought, and just to ruin your first day. Anyway, the fellow had been all messed about. His head was just blood and flies. Rabble.' Smith stopped talking because they had reached the Phoenicia.

The photographers jumped out but Smith and Adam stayed in their places. A red glow lit the rim of the crater on the Corniche and, silhouetted against the glow, figures were firing like demons into the depths. Adam closed his eyes.

'You fags can speak this language . . .'

'Come and translate this crap . . .'

Adam got out. He kept his eyes shut but the glow came in through his closed eyelids. He put his hand to his nose but smelt the unspeakable barbecue. On the rim of the crater, he looked down on flames twisting and curling round legs and arms. He saw an empty blue petrol tin and a placard scrawled with Arabic. His foot dislodged some earth, which rolled down towards a burning arm. He carefully kicked some more down on to the burning arm, which was missing its hand.

'What does that say . . .'

'Come on, man . . .'

'It says.' Adam coughed up whisky. 'It says: So perish traitors.' One of the boys stopped firing and caught him because he was being sick, whisky and cigarettes and Club Special Port and the memory of Hussein Sarabi with his gentle voice.

'Oh hard cheese,' said Smith, taking him back to the jeep.

'*Nunc dimittis*.'

'That's Latin, isn't it? Never did any. Father was a bookie.'

'At Catford . . .'

'How did you know? My brother does the book now. Buys dogs out of selling-plates. What a life!'

'Ah,' said Adam. 'Brother. Not you.'

'Can't you . . .'

'. . . Can it . . .'

CHAPTER TWELVE

'I have found the man.'

'Which man, Said? Which man?' Adam was so tired and Said could be so irritating.

It was the seventh or the eighth ceasefire. Hassan would not budge on the point about taking their heavy weapons. His left eye twitched like Oliver's. '*Régime de douche écossaise,*' said M. Le Président with a broad gesture and Adam wrote the words down though the great man's breath stank of a sweet liqueur. '*La bataille de Beyrouth aura lieu. Ce Sharon là-bas . . .*'

Adam was so tired. He drank Turkish coffee obsessively. He would sleep for an hour in the afternoon but not at all at night, hearing through the wall Smith talking to himself. ('Who is right? Tell me that. Take the IDF. They're all right, the reserve officers, fine soldiers and regular blokes. And the PLO? Who would have thought they could fight like this? . . . They'll put in the air force. Or no. They'll come in at the Museum. That much is straight. Up Corniche Mazraa. Cut the city in half. What happens then? Do these maniacs fall back on the hotel and hide behind us? Interesting!') Adam never shut him up. He merely lay in bed, smoking and drinking beer from his warm fridge, till the call to morning prayer told him it was light.

Omar was dead. That much was straight. Killed in the bombardment of Borj al-Brajnie. Poor, smiling Omar. And Kate? Adam went down on the morning of the eighth (or was it the ninth?) ceasefire but she was in the Intensive Care room *arg beschäftigt*, and please, please could Mr Adam come back when she had less work. The upper floors of the hospital had been evacuated, the kitchen feeding the whole quarter. And Johnny? Somewhere; somewhere in this great

153

city which is dying of apathy, dying of people sitting all day on their balconies and staring out to sea, dying of rats and wild dogs and rubbish that nobody bothers to burn any more, dying of despair shot through with panic.

The blockade was lifted. The blockade came down. Jaffa oranges filled the stalls on Hamra Street; or, returning one afternoon, Smith and Adam found notes in their pigeonholes from the IDF, ribbing them for unbalanced coverage and inviting them to lunch at Baabda. Smith went; Adam did not. For was it not already in their midst? Car bombs devastated refugee centres, militiamen shot their officers, a consignment of flour was burned because of worms. The vanguard was among them; yet quizzing the stall-holders or the Admiral front desk, or moving quickly from door to door on carpets of box-leaves and flesh and glass, Adam found he was always too late.

The water was turned on. The water was turned off. 'They'll come in at the Museum,' the photographers said at breakfast and Jauhara dropped a pile of plates. Smith knocked them down. Smith apologised. Smith said he was considering getting a gun, the price was tumbling, but no Soviet rubbish. What for, said Adam. For the crisis, said Smith.

'Which man, Said?' The boy could be so infuriating and Adam was so tired.

'The man who is watching you.'

'Oh my God. Let's go to the Museum. I mean,' Adam stopped. 'What should we do, Said?'

'He was watching you in Hamra when United Press was hit and then he followed you to Reuter and waited. This is very dangerous.'

'Said, what can we do?'

'I have one gun in the back. 1400 liras only. Everybody is becoming a civilian.'

'Oh Said, I asked you not to.' Then Adam remembered something. Was it this year or last year? 'Do you remember that armed element, your friend, in Sodeco? Let us find him.' Adam felt better as they drove towards the Green Line. It was all this drinking, coffee by day and whisky by night.

The boy had not lost his shyness and sat uncomfortably in the back, cradling his AK-47 on his knees. Soviet rubbish, Adam thought and then remembered something from last year.

'My dear, tell me about that sharpshooter last year.' Adam looked round.

'I cannot, please, I cannot. He wore one mask.'

'I understand,' said Adam, looking at him gently. 'But you knew he was an agent for the enemy.'

'No, no, how can I know? Maybe, for Syria. To cause one incident.'

Adam felt sorry for the boy. 'My dear, what was his weapon? That you must know.'

'It was Israel M-sixteen. But this you can find in the city, in every stall here in Hamra.'

'Of course. And you are kind to help us now.'

Said tried to park in Hamra Street.

'No parking. No parking.' A fat man got up from his chair and loped towards them. He wore a tee-shirt marked *Newsweek. Do not shoot! Ne Tirez Pas!* and then 'Press' underneath in Arabic. 'Please your passport.'

'Come on. You know me. You were captain at the hotel. We're not a car bomb.'

'I am now security organ of this sector. Where is your passport?'

It was not a large sector, for there was a formal check-point of the Palestine Armed Struggle Command twenty yards ahead and the ridiculous Pink Panthers, their uniforms patterned with tanks, the same distance behind. The sector embraced, Adam noted vaguely, old M. Habib's closed tailoring business and two stalls selling, respectively, cheap Israeli shirts and candles and batteries. Adam took out the four pieces of Hassan's pass, crumpled and run with sweat, and held them together carefully.

'Where are the warriors?'

'They are stiffening other important fronts. Your pass is many weeks out of date.'

Said and the armed element ignored the security organ and got out of the car. Adam watched them as far as an orange-juice shop where they stopped and spoke into its door. A boy with a baby-blue tee-shirt and a bead necklace stepped out into the sunlight and shook hands with the armed element. Adam took back his pass and walked towards them. The security organ followed.

Said intercepted them in the middle of the road. 'He says he has a message from your friend.'

'Which friend?' Was it siege-inflation of the word or was it fact: Adam now seemed to have many friends. Kate, he thought suddenly and the thought was pleasant to him; but they would not call her friend but a lady. 'Let me speak to the boy.'

Adam crossed the road, the lonely security organ loping after him. Curiously, the boy was much less tense than that first time, outside the Research Institute, last year.

'Is this the man? Tell him I have a message from his brother.'

'Tell me now, my dear.'

'He says, your brother says,' and the boy looked skywards, 'he says that you must leave the city. The situation is bad. Your leaving is better for you and also for him. He wishes you well and also his beloved sister.'

'Will he leave? This is my question and also her wish.'

'Only to Palestine,' the boy said sententiously and then turned and spoke hurriedly to Said, too quickly for Adam to understand.

'Let's go,' said Said.

'What was the other message? It is important for me!'

Said shrugged and spoke to the boy. 'He, your friend, says that Palestine is . . .' Said turned and interrogated the boy once again. 'He says that Palestine is a piece of your brain.'

'Don't be so stupid, Said.'

'Your heart,' said the security organ. 'A condition of your heart.' Other voices chimed in. Adam spun round and saw a knot of armed elements, including the PASC men and the Pink Panthers, had formed about them. He raised his arms impatiently for order.

'Tell me the Arabic directly, but slowly.'

The boy in blue began again the difficult sentence.

'Ah,' said Adam and walked back towards the car. He

thanked their armed element who refused, with ill-disguised relief, a lift back to his post.

'What is the message?' Said seemed hurt.

'It is an English expression. Let us go to Gaza Hospital.'

'Tell me first.'

'It was: Palestine is a state of mind.'

Said looked at him dubiously.

'It means, dear Said, that your home is where you think it is, where you belong.'

'True,' said Said and looked at him sadly. 'So you will leave. This is not your home.'

'Maybe. Let us go to Gaza now so we can return before night.'

Why not go today? They are stepping up their military pressure. Maybe the battle will begin at last.' He was crying now.

'That's enough, Said.'

'I'll take you to the Museum now, if you want. You will not come back.'

'That's enough, I said. Take me to Gaza. Drop me there.'

Never fix a date, Lukomski had said; just get up and go. That is what they had learned in Vietnam. Short time, the men called it, when the date comes through in the last month of the tour and everything goes, no good for anything, because there is the date and a bullet will come between the men and the date. Said stopped in Fakhani so Adam could be sick. He was always being sick now because of the coffee.

Kate was in the little doctors' common room, sitting back in a chair with her eyes closed. She opened them and clapped the palms of her hands together when Adam took a small step towards her.

'I knew you would come back.'

'*Ich grüsse dich*.' Adam looked down to the bandage on her wrist.

'Oh, that is an abcess. I do not understand. It will not heal. But I am so happy that you came. Do you want to see our work? Dr Khaled studied in Leeds.'

'I like to try and speak German, Kate. But aren't you busy?'

157

'Not now. We are working only 10 per cent capacity. It is when the bombs come that the whole house bleeds.' She laughed and looked at him through long eyelashes he had not noticed that first time. 'Why do you call me that name?'

'Short for Katyusha. That is how we met at the American hospital.'

'That is nice,' she said doubtfully. 'But you must not let the others hear. The situation is very bad. People cannot do as they please. Miss Dr Samira is my name.'

'Kate,' he said.

They climbed seven flights of stairs to the top floor, Miss Dr Samira leading the way with her white coat billowing out behind her. Warm evening sunlight slanted into the gutted rooms and Adam could see a quiet sea through the wounds left by shellfire. A 50-kilogram bomb had come in through the roof, just at the point where Dr Khaled had had painted a red cross.

'You cannot always blame the cousins,' she said and laughed. 'The anti-aircraft guns send the machines upward and so they miss.' She pointed out the stains on the walls from phosphorus.

'We have two sets of problems and this you must understand when you write. The first comes from the war and the second from the blockade.'

Adam had difficulty keeping up with her as she hurried from room to room. He needed to stop, translate, write in his notebook, and there she was, at the end of the empty ward, beckoning.

'The first is, of course, the casualties from the new weapons the cousins are using. Dr Khaled says they have completely altered the old ratio of wound to kill.

'Second. Three patients killed in here on the first Friday.' They had reached the second floor. Adam had to break into a run to catch her.

'Second.' This was the first floor. 'Here is the intensive care. Second; these are the problems of the blockade. I have no mains electricity so I can have no lift for the patients, no dry-heat sterilization and no blood bank because, as you know, blood must be kept at a steady 4 degrees and our generator is wavering. The water pipe was broken when they bombed the Cité Sportive so I must wash everything in the well, even my overall. This is not clean.'

She held out her hands to Adam. 'Even these disposable gloves I have washed.' Adam reached out to take her right hand but she quickly turned round.

They entered the ward. Behind a glass partition, there were six patients, except there was not any glass in the partition and the windows were blocked on the land side by sandbags.

'More slowly, please, Kate. This German is hard for me.'

'Of course. My problem here is sepsis. But I have not the antibiotics for prophylactic use. Sometimes I want to weep because I cannot stop sepsis.' She looked up at Adam. He wanted to put his arms around her.

'But Dr Hoffmann always said it was a matter of priority. We are now doing life saving and organ saving but otherwise, the old people with chest ailments, what Dr Khaled calls the hidden victims . . .'

'Who is Dr Hoffmann?'

'He was my professor in Leipzig. He was a good man. For example, we use air instead of oxygen; wounds to the kidney, take out the organ; wounds to extremities, amputate. Do you understand? Only the worst cases here.'

The patients were divided by a second partition, one and five. Amid the larger group was a child entirely swathed in bandages. Adam looked away into the bright evening sunshine.

'Ah. From Borj al-Brajnie. Unknown No. 72. Tracheostomy. About 30 per cent chance but I am worried about chest infection.'

Adam avoided the child but his look passed through into the other section. A young man was propped upright in a chair with tubes passing into his head. Miss Dr Samira followed Adam's gaze.

'Very bad case.'

'Military?'

'The young men usually are. I have done a craniotomy but there is acute bleeding under the skin. Maybe 10 per cent but paralysed completely.'

'Oh dear . . .'

'I think these patients make you sad. Do you want to see obstetrics?'

Adam looked at her and she blushed all over. She looked down at the floor.

'Do you know what Adam means in Arabic?'

'Yes. *Mensch*. Human being. But it's Hebrew as much as Arabic.'

'Of course.' She looked up, her blush gone. 'It is now our national duty to produce children. Cousin Sharon is making my colleagues' work easy. During the first bombardment, three women gave birth in the street. Premature, of course, but mother and child healthy.'

'Kate . . .'

'It is getting worse. Soon, maybe, I will be performing operations by candle light like Ibn Sina. But we cannot stop. Excuse me.' She turned her back on him. Adam thought she was about to cry.

'I must leave you. I have to drain some fluid from this patient's brain. Do not watch, if it makes you unhappy.'

Adam turned and looked through the blasted windows on the sea side. A glorious sunset was beginning, the red sun dipping to melt and reform over the ruined Cité Sportive. He turned again. He should leave before dark but the slanting rays were edging her coat and hair with red and gold as she worked. At her feet were a few drops of blood. Their eyes crossed and she stared down in embarrassment and irritation.

'I'll clean it,' he said, opening the door.

She sprang towards him. 'No. You can't come in here, Adam. This is the Green Line. You are not sterile. It is a principle.'

Adam turned back to the sea side. When she had finished, he would put his arms around her and they would drop to the ground and sleep till the war was over.

She stood, golden, before the partition, her eyes closed from the sun.

'Kate, can I say something?'

'No, please.' She took a step back but her eyes were still closed.

'Kate, you are the most beautiful and the bravest woman . . .'

'No, no,' she said. 'You do not understand. First, I am not a woman, but a girl. Second, the situation is bad. People cannot do as they wish. This is, so to speak, *jahinnom*.'

'Hell,' he said and fell to his knees. Something hit him painfully on the shoulder. It was a panel, from the false ceiling. Car bomb, he thought automatically, about 15 kilograms. There was ragged firing, but heavier and slower than usual. The Palestinians want to travel light, he thought; they are shooting off their heavy ammunition. Then he remembered something. 'That was how we met, darling Kate. In Sanaya Garden. That big car bomb. My first day.' He looked into her black eyes and saw that strange, compassionate look he remembered from Johnny in Rouche and something more: anxiety, perhaps, or need.

'You are incorrect. This is not a car bomb. This is a *Luftangriff*. It is very dangerous.'

'Oh my darling.' He could hear the engines now, coming in so fast from the sea side, over the hospital, and the heavy flak from in front. 'Oh my sweet Kate, what do we do?'

'Don't do that with your teeth. I cannot do dentistry.' She touched him gently on the face and, as she touched him, he felt all his strength run out of him and then a flash lit the landward windows and they went onto their knees. There was a moment's silence; then the sandbags shook and burst and the partition door sprang open.

'Give me something to do.' He was holding her tight. 'Do you want blood? I am B negative . . .'

'No, you need your strength to write this story.' She got up, putting his arm through hers.

'Help carry these patients down?'

'No. They are too ill to be moved. They are in God's hands.' She closed the partition door gently. 'Let us go downstairs and wait for the poor people. The emergency room is there.'

Virgin of the Dog River, angel of armies, we have reached the stairs; and here it comes now, the engines, flash, silence, thank God there is no glass; get up; if they were hit, they would not hear the explosion, like that first day at

161

Sanava; but what are all these people doing? Don't they know the hospital isn't safe and this old woman, she's mad, she has framed snapshots in each hand. No, I have not seen them; get away from me, you . . .

'Adam,' said Miss Dr Samira sharply. 'It is better to try and hide your fear. Take the poor people down to the basement.' A tap on the shoulder made Adam spin round. It was Dr Khaled.

This is better. This way, madam. Careful with the steps. No, not the lift. It does not work. There is no electricity. Here it comes again; Jesus, it's closer; down, it says, down; and the dust and the paper. Get up. All right. Sweet Kate, you are everything to me, mother and mate. Wailing. That's an ambulance. No, come downstairs, old man, you are in the doctors' way and it is safer below. Yes, that's right, clear the doorway, there where she is standing, on the other side of the door; and here it comes, but I am standing; and the ambulance and the boys are running in and Kate is over the stretcher, oh dear, the blood; a cigarette; they've taken off his boots, his feet are white, his face is as white as paper. Poor old Johnny.

'Let me help.' Adam put a hand to the stretcher as they ran for the emergency room. 'He is my friend.'

'Put that cigarette out,' she whispered. 'You have no medical knowledge, Adam.' My God, that's close. Even she's on her knees. They can only make one pass. Because of fuel. My leg. It's all bloody. No, that's Johnny. Cigarette. No. Dr Khaled and a European nurse are working on a second patient through the dust.

'Let me stay with him, Kate.' She is cutting away at the left trouser leg. His eyes are closed. He looks absurd. So white in that green uniform. Take his hand. It is so cold.

'We were at Oxford University together.' She has got the trouser clear now and is cleaning at the wound. Nothing left of the thigh, really, only wound. And here it comes, a flash that obliterates the sun.

'Get up, Adam. Go to the basin, wash your hands and put on the gloves. Then hold the instruments for me so I can see what I need. Unfortunately, we have only one nurse.'

This is better. Doing something useful now. She is

picking out the cloth and speaking: 'I would like to go to Oxford University or to Leeds to learn English and study psychiatry. You understand we have many mental problems with our people. How much would it cost for me to live one year in Oxford, including food?'

'Oh Kate, what a question.' Adam looked down at her, smiling. He wanted to touch her. 'My God, Kate, they're crazy, they've brought a gun up.' The heavy reports shook the ground at his feet. 'Can't we stop them?'

Without turning round, she raised her left hand and touched him on the arm. 'Adam, you must keep calm if you are to work with us. Dr Khaled will speak with the boys. It has happened before. You understand, they want to be here too.' Adam looked up and only the nurse was visible through the dust.

'They brought an Israeli here,' she said quietly. The anti-aircraft fire had stopped and Adam now wanted it back. 'The boys were angry and firing their guns but Dr Khaled told them not to be foolish. There was damage to the neck and spinal jarring, I think from leaving the machine when it was hit. No burns. He made good progress although he was frightened of us at the beginning.'

Johnny Penrose opened his tired blue eyes. 'I thought I told you to leave.' He tried to smile.

'You did. But Johnny, you've been hit in the leg. *Wie schwer, darf ich ihm sagen?*' This must be shellfire now. No; there is the flash and will it never stop?

'Tell him it is simple wounding of the upper left thigh. I had feared poly trauma as is usual with cluster.'

'Could have been much worse, Johnny. We'll go out, all of us, when Kate has put you together. We won't tell anybody. We'll go to Syria, Yemen, Tunisia, who cares? I'll look after you and Kate will come . . .'

'I thought I told you to leave.' His eyes had become vague and without lustre. His hair was white with dust.

'But, Johnny . . .'

'Don't you understand yet?'

'*Ruhe mal.*'

'You mustn't talk, Johnny.'

'But don't you understand yet? You're bringing them to

me. Just as with Lukomski. They don't care about you. They might even let you across.' Johnny Penrose closed his eyes. 'Why not try it? Alone. For the first time in your life.'

Adam took a step back and felt the world lose its shape.

'Stand up. Into the basin. That is better.' Kate had him by the shoulder. 'Do not worry. Your friend has psychological problems. That is usual after a bad wound. But you see you must leave. The boys are taking Dr Khaled's patient to AUH. You go with them in the ambulance.'

'Kate . . .'

'You must leave. I will now perform an operation.' The nurse joined her, smiling at Adam. She was German.

'Oh my God, you're not going to cut the leg off.'

'You have no medical knowledge, Adam. There is massive tissue and bone damage. You must leave. You are disturbing our work.'

Adam walked to the door.

'I'm sorry, Adam, but we are so busy. You must not come back, please.' He looked round. She was crying as she worked.

'What shall I say to Dr Hoffmann?'

'Tell him.' The nurse brought up a screen and concealed herself, Kate and Johnny. 'Tell him. Adam, tell him this.'

Adam found the ambulance in the burning street.

CHAPTER THIRTEEN

Adam crossed at the Museum, just after dawn. Smith had wavered a moment but decided, really, that he should stay a couple more days: the Palestinians looked as if they had got the message, though they had fought, in the end, hadn't they? He had never really felt at home on the other side and he was Boutros' hostage for 5,000 pounds.

Adam and Said drank a last beer together. Said had brought his grief under control and in the final reckoning, as to how much Boutros would advance him against Adam's word, he pointed out that benzine was now 70 liras a litre. Adam said he would return and embraced the boy while the fighters dozed by the last earthwork and Cerberus urinated on the wheels. Then Said got back in and with a flourish and a squeal of tyres turned the big red car round and sped back into the waking city.

This is how it begins, crossing at the Museum. Last year, blue jacarandas were in flower but these trees are orange-red; and there are no birds in the trees; no singing birds even among the French Ambassador's decapitated pines.

Past the Palais de Justice. My back is wide; my chest is wide; but it does not matter any more, because there is nothing between them. Past the Palais Mansour, where . . .

Adam tripped and sprawled forward and Toby's suitcase executed a messy arc, fell and sprang open. Adam sat down in the rubble and began to laugh and, then, after a while, to cry. He went on sitting and crying, while a little breeze ruffled the pages of his notebooks, blew away the four squares of Hassan's pass, now ten years out of date, and sprinkled greasy red petals around him.

'You cannot sit here. This is a bad place. Sharpshooters.'

The driver had backed onto the crossing and was hurriedly gathering up Adam's things.

'Sorry.' Adam got into the car. The driver handed him a paper handkerchief and a comb.

'Where go?'

The Kataib officers were laughing so much they did not even ask for Adam's passport.

'Go Alexandre Hotel? Go Kataib HQ? Go IDF?' Adam combed and combed his hair.

'Go IDF?'

'Go IDF.'

As they climbed up to Baabda, it became deliciously cool. The air smelled of hay and fruit and Israeli soldiers wandered among the shops or stood quite still in the road, trying to count their change. At the roundabout, Adam looked down the long, straight, empty road past Galerie Semaan and saw the red earth in its mouth.

The driver stopped in a dusty square before the Conservatoire. There was an unfinished, suburban air about the place. Cast blocks of concrete lay among the weeds and jeeps were parked in neat rows, with orange polythene on their roofs to identify them to aircraft.

'Hi. I'm Uri. Colonel Paul is off today and I'm standing in for him. For what it's worth.' He was a large man with a skull cap on his black, curly hair and he towered over his desk.

'Adam Murray. *DT*. Hi.'

'Can't say I've seen your stuff, but then we don't get the papers up here. I read it back home, in Hemel Hempstead. I'm a GP.'

'If you're a doctor, why are you killing all these people?'

Colonel Uri looked at Adam in surprise.

'Sorry. Please forgive me. I'm afraid West Beirut is rather a . . .' Adam had forgotten the word.

'It's the war. Nothing you or I can do about it. You look bushed. Can I get you a drink?'

'Please.'

It would be whisky; a stiff, military tot of whisky.

Colonel Uri set a plastic mug beside him. It was water. Like Dives, Adam thought.

'Another?'

'Please.'

The officer seemed to tire of acting as Adam's cupbearer for he sat down behind his desk and picked up a form.

'Well, here's the procedure, Adam. You're not going anywhere today. Sabbath begins at sunset and the border is closed. You also have to give 48 hours notice. I'm afraid it looks like Monday. You'll have to sit in Achrafiyeh for a day or two.'

'Like Purgatory.'

'What?'

'Sorry.'

An immense figure blocked the door, unsteady from the sunlight. It wore a brown safari suit and the freckled neck and face were raw with sunburn. Beside it was a young man with a clumsy motion of his left shoulder and an epaulette marked Security. 'Not a bad effort, I felt,' it said.

THREE

THE PEACE OF JERUSALEM

CHAPTER FOURTEEN

Sir Donald Penrose and his daughter were waiting on the quay as the steamer pulled within the shelter of the mole.

A small crowd had gathered to watch the arrival of the weekly boat, but Adam was the only passenger to disembark. The others were bound for the larger islands: Colonsay, Islay, Jura, Mull. As Adam limped down the gangplank with his new Achrafiyeh suitcase, Sir Donald opened his arms wide. 'Hail to the returning hero,' he said.

Laura grasped his arm tightly. 'All right. I couldn't stand it. Alive.'

They walked down the mole towards a battered car.

'And Johnny?' Laura was still holding his arm.

'All right. Alive.'

She seemed to want to question him further but thought better of it and they squeezed into the hopeless car and set off along a tarmacked road which soon degenerated into track. Adam glanced round and the people were now watching the steamer pull out.

'I'm afraid Oddjob's here,' she said softly. They were crossing a bog.'

'Laura, why?'

'Because Mary wouldn't come otherwise. Oh Adam, I'm so worried about her. Please help me.'

They rattled to the brow of a little hill and descended into a green valley. It was closed at both ends. Corn fields stood ready for cutting and a sturdy pink eighteenth-century house appeared in its own little park of oaks.

'But Laura, I expected something wild and flinty.'

'The wind doesn't come in too much,' said Sir Donald. 'Only the rain.'

The spaniels emerged desperately from the front door as

the old car was silenced. If anything, the house was even tattier than Kent, though work had begun on a new wing. Persian rugs lay askew on the panelled floors and the pictures, which might have been Raeburn, might have been Gainsborough, looked underfed, the frames flaking, the canvas loose. Ropes and other sailing paraphernalia lay piled around the walls.

'Have some breakfast,' said Sir Donald, leading the way into the dining-room. 'Some of the party are fasting.'

The first thing Adam saw in the room was the portrait of Laura's mother from Kent, with those big black eyes with their spark which reminded him of somebody else, some time ago. Beneath the picture, a small figure in a striped Jermyn Street dressing gown was helping itself furtively from the hot plate.

'Oliver!' said Sir Donald. Oliver looked round, startled. His head was covered with fuzz as if the damp climate had brought on his new hair. 'I understood you were on the boiled-rice regimen.'

'Yes, but . . .'

'Yes, Oliver. You're either ill or you aren't.' There was a little hardness in Laura's voice.

Sir Donald turned on Adam. 'Only I am on a full diet. My darling has made the most progress and has a cooked breakfast. I take it you will be on boiled rice, because of the war.'

'Well, I rather went off meat during the siege. But I'm feeling better.'

Sir Donald looked at him sadly. 'If you're sure, help yourself. But I think boiled rice at midday, at least for the first few days. I'll tell Mrs Eggins so she knows.'

'I'm sorry you're not feeling well, Oliver.' Adam sat down opposite him but he took no notice, dully stirring his boiled rice round his plate. 'Look. Oliver. I'm sorry for taking a swing at you in Ireland.'

'What?' Oliver blinked at him.

Adam gave up. 'Where's Mary?'

'She comes down for lunch,' said Laura, looking hard at Adam.

'Should I go up?'

'I wouldn't,' said Oliver.

Sir Donald returned from the kitchen and predicted a bad storm. Laura and Adam went out for a walk while the weather held. She put on four heavy jumpers that entirely concealed her shape and covered it all in a shiny red mackintosh. The spaniels bounded off with them across the little park but soon lost heart.

'What a lovely place, Log. You are lucky.' The corn was full of seabirds Adam had never seen before and large birds of prey circled the high tops.

'But it's so hopeless. The people have nothing to do. They won't fish. Farming doesn't pay. We haven't got any money and the tourists don't like the weather. Papa tried to start a factory for tinning fish and another for weaving but they didn't work. The people go down to the jetty and watch the steamer or sit in the pub and drink whisky.'

'What will happen?'

'I'm not leaving.' She turned on him and blocked his way. Her town shoes and stockings were wet from the grass. 'We'll keep it going somehow. If only Johnny . . .' She stopped in embarrassment. 'Do you want to talk about it, the war?'

Adam helped her over the iron palings which separated the park from the cornfields. 'Not much. I didn't really distinguish myself.'

'But we saw the pictures on the television, every day, always burning and we didn't know where Johnny was. Or you.'

'Johnny's in good hands.'

She looked at him closely.

'Look, Log. Johnny and I had a flaming row. That's what besieging armies do. They put up walls between friends. He'll be all right.'

'But Papa is so gloomy. I think he's giving up hope. He sort of thought you might bring him back.'

'I tried.' He put his arm through hers and then removed it.

'And then he was so depressed about poor Jocelyn Ambrose.'

173

'Milan's a rough town, Log. Especially in that sort of world.'

'But to run him over after? The papers said they couldn't identify his face at first.'

'Let's not talk about it.'

They turned back to the house. She stopped and blocked his way again. 'Why did it all happen? First Toby. And Mary so ill. And Johnny miles away. And poor, poor Jolly. Why did everything go wrong?'

'I don't really know yet. How long have I got?'

'Oh Adam, it's not a penance. As long as you like. Three weeks. Four weeks. Why are you limping, anyway?'

'I got plastered and fell down the stairs at the Admiral.'

'Adam, can you never be sensible? And don't call me Log in front of the others.'

Mary was stepping gently down the stairs as they went in. She had become so thin and pale that the light seemed to shine through her. She wore a dress with full sleeves to the wrist.

'You look lovely, Mary. But so thin.'

She smiled bleakly and offered her cheek for a kiss. 'Poor Adam has looked into the heart of darkness. What did you see?' She smiled and went ahead into lunch.

Only Sir Donald and Adam ate and talked at lunch. Sir Donald made no mention of Johnny but asked concrete and accurate questions about the city. Adam's replies were short, for he did not wish to bore the others. He was thinking, too, as he ate his boiled rice or cast glances at Mary, smoking, or Laura trembling under her mother's portrait, of the questions they had posed him. What had he seen? What had gone wrong?

He had seen what he had expected to see, the skin of civilisation peeled away, the executions in the crater, the mutinies in the garrison, the esurient rats. But going down, down, down, down, which is the sound the bombs make, he touched with his foot something firm and safe. Johnny will not see Palestine. Kate will not see Palestine; but where was she when she drained the fluid from that fighter's skull or clipped at the young man's bloody trousers? In Sabra. But Sabra was destroyed. The Red Cross said it was unfit for human habitation, abandoned by all but the poor and the mad. Kate was not poor, not mad. She was at home in Gaza.

Perhaps the answer to the other question lay nearby. Adam reached out for it but Sir Donald was repeating his question about the defences at the Museum.

After lunch, Adam followed Mary to her room. She sat down on the bed and looked away.

'I'm sorry for going off,' he said.

'We could try again, you know. It might not be too late.'

The barometer was sinking, as Sir Donald hourly reported, and by dinner a great storm had sprung up. Adam lay in her bed, thinking to hear in the thunder the sound of engines and bombs and to see in the lightning the blinding flares against heat-seeking rockets. In the morning, she said quietly that she was not sleeping well and that he had talked constantly in some foreign language. Adam wondered if it was the marks on his feet which upset her. He spent the next night in his own room.

All that week Beirut burned. Adam sat before the television for the evening news and they would ask him, where is that and where is that? Adam could not tell. The film was taken from a high building on the eastern side, the Alexandre Hotel perhaps. Everything looked the same at that distance. That ruined apartment block: was that Rouche? Was that Hamra?

They came in at the Museum early one morning, screaming for people to run for their lives, but boys with RPGs disabled the tank tracks and the bulldozers and they retired, stunned, as if from the heat of a great fire. They sat on the hills, morosely firing at everything, the Bristol, the Admiral, Hamra Street, till the Palestinians woke in agony from their walking dream and gave up their last condition. Smith, questioned by some miracle of telecommunications from his burned-out room, said the city had lost its hatred for the Palestinians and had come, in a curious way, to respect them. Adam smiled but said nothing.

It was sunny but windy. Adam and Laura played tennis with one ball, spinning a coin for the end with the dead patch. Sir Donald sailed them round the island through fields of gannets and seals scattered like footballs on the water till the boat approached and they sank with a gurgle. A date was set for the departure of the fighters to Syria, Yemen, Tunisia.

They bathed in the swimming pool built by the islanders. Mary would lie naked on the grass, her hand resting neatly in her groin, her eyes half-open and her mouth half-closed, her right arm covered by a towel. Oliver sat some distance away by a laurel bush and peered at her furtively. Laura wore voluminous bathing dresses and swam up and down, her head erect, her hair dry. Bachir, Lebanon's hope, was elected President in a parliament ringed by his men.

Oliver telephoned the mainland. In his intervals, Adam tried to reach Leipzig but without success. However, the postmistress's son, who was helping Sir Donald reshelve the library according to the Dewey system, found him an old manual of German letter-writing and he composed a courtly letter to Dr Hoffmann, imploring him to press his thumbs for his *Sorgenkind* in whom he could feel well pleased. The fighters left the city in brand-new uniforms, a credit to the mothers of Borj al-Brajnie, waving their weapons. Adam sat close to the television but did not see anyone he knew except the officer from Galerie Semaan, with a head wound, marshalling his men.

Laura showed Adam a hill loch. There were no paths to it and they kept sinking into bog as they walked. The boat-house was crumbling with age and air and salt but, from the middle of the loch, the sheet of water gave way, uninter-rupted, to the unending sea as if they were floating on a staircase to heaven. Beside the boathouse, a single alder was coming into leaf as if Adam's long summer was never to end. Adam fished. The trout were small and wild and Adam did not know how they had come to be there. When hooked, they fought with a fury for a minute and then went heavy on the line as if they were weary of the place. As Adam brought them up, they showed for a moment all the colours of their lost medium. One he killed: but Mrs Eggins so covered it with batter that he ground off the barbs of his hooks with Mary's nail-file and released them all gently. He tried a dry fly but they rose always short of the fly as if contact with the air was appalling to them. Bachir, Lebanon's hope, was killed by a car bomb.

In the evenings, the Penroses, Mrs Eggins and Adam played bad bridge. Sir Donald always overbid and Laura always underbid, so to partner either was to run up futile overtricks or be doubled into oblivion. Mrs Eggins, who played well and for whom these uncompleted rubbers must have been torture, always complimented them on their play. The Israelis crossed, unopposed, at the Museum.

Mary would lie by the fire while Oliver spoke to her of his future. He had to return to London, on business, but would not wait for the weekly steamer. He would return, after only two days away, and, the excitement of it, by helicopter! Recruits from the pub started to build a circle of stones as a landing ground in the park but lost interest and drifted away. Laura, who would come to sit on Adam's bed in the morning, begged him to do something. Boutros was arrested but was hurriedly released when all three American networks played the story prominently.

'Ah, Oliver. Can I have a word with you?'

Mary was by the swimming pool, Laura asleep in the television room, Sir Donald demolishing a dry-stone wall for the men to rebuild. Oliver replaced the telephone receiver.

'Look, Oliver. I wonder if you really need go. I'm worried about Mary. I think she ought to have a break from that stuff.'

Oliver began to twitch. 'What do you mean?'

'Look, old boy, we don't have to act a part any more, you know. The situation is bad. People can't do what they like.'

'I don't understand you, Adam. You don't make sense. You're shell-shocked or something. Mary thinks so.' He picked up the receiver and started to dial.

'You'll kill her. Look at her arms.'

'What do you know about it? When she needed you, you just ran off to play at being a hero. This stuff is all right. I can take it or leave it. You just have to know how to pace yourself.'

'What does that mean?'

'Adam. Adam.' Laura ran into the room, in bare feet, her

blue eyes staring. 'Come quickly. Something awful has happened. On the television.'

'I'm terribly sorry, Sir Donald. I'll try and replace them in Oban. I'll go over on the steamer.'

'It's all right.' Sir Donald put his arm round Adam's shoulder. 'Have some more breakfast, unless you want to go back on boiled rice. I'll tell Mrs Eggins. Laura says you knew the nurse.'

'She wasn't a nurse. She was a neurosurgeon. She was the bravest and the . . .' Adam stopped and drank his tea.

'Why did they do it? Why did they let those beasts into the camps?'

'It was the place, Sir Donald. They thought they could go through the Museum and stay the same. But you can't.'

'I loved a lady once.' Sir Donald looked at Adam shyly. His gaze passed over Adam's head.

Adam did not turn round. 'It's not that. You must understand, Sir Donald. I only told Butterworth that so that they would leave him alone. She stayed with her patients on the first floor. She would never leave them. But you read Smith's piece. The walking patients . . .' Adam stopped.

'She was beautiful like Laura. But she went away. To Africa.'

'Sir Donald, you must believe me. It didn't hurt very much, what they were doing. And they stopped when I said that, because that's what he wanted to hear. And Jolly. Milan is a rough town. You know that.'

'She went away.' Sir Donald extended an open hand. 'Let's go out to the park. We would not want to miss the great event.'

Out in the park, they could hear the machine approaching and young men were running through the fields. As it landed, it blew the first dying leaves off the oaks. A lady emerged and stood under the blades so that her skirt blew over her head, revealing short legs in stockings. The young men turned away and looked up at the eagles absently. She waited for Oliver and then came forward, smoothing down her dress with one arm, saw Adam and then settled on Sir Donald. They both took a step back.

'I've heard so much about you from Ollie,' she said.

'Come, my dear, and have some breakfast. I would imagine, after London and your flight, that you are not ready for . . .'

'So you brought Poppy as well,' said Adam to Oliver quietly.

'What do you mean, as well? You don't make sense, Adam.'

Laura hissed at Adam through a second sitting of breakfast. Poppy had hurt her foot stepping out of the helicopter and could Sir Donald help her with her shoes? She was offered boiled rice, because of the injured foot. Could Sir Donald, please, help her with the window sash and the electric fire in her bedroom? She went onto boiled rice. Mary was excused lunch.

Adam went up to the loch. On an island was a ruined house but when Adam landed to visit it, he found it was not ruined, merely started and never finished.

Mary emerged that evening and turned one cool, empty look on the unfortunate Poppy. Poppy, it seemed, was expected at David's and really ought to take the next steamer over. David had taken his lodge on Speyside where only he of his large house-party was ever lucky enough to get into the salmon and only he had the good fortune of a fluky neck shot at the end of a long stalk.

Adam went up to the loch. He would go after breakfast, even when it rained, and occasionally a red speck would appear on the hill and he would row to shore. He kept two jumpers in the boathouse. She would sit quite silently in the bow, huddled against the gusts of wind, while Adam cast ever more accurately and quietly with his sharp, unbarbed hooks.

The telephone kept saying that Mary (and Adam) were expected at David's. The salmon were running and the stags had come down from the hill. Henry would meet her, them both, at Oban.

'You're not going to David's with Mary and Oddjob?' she said suddenly one day.

179

'No, are you?' Adam cast.

'Oh Adam. So that's the end, isn't it?' The wind drove a cloud across the sun and ruffled the water into little waves. The place became cold and dark.

'Yes.'

'So what now?'

The sun reappeared and, for a moment, the place was friendly and hospitable. Then the water blew up into waves and the sun vanished.

'Away.'

'Please don't.

She was huddled against the wind, a shapeless mass of wool and plastic mackintosh. Her eyes had lost their colour.

Adam looked away to cast again. 'Why not come? We ought to stick together, in a way.' The line sank and he started gently pulling it in.

'Oh Adam.'

'I hadn't known till I came to the island. Silly, isn't it?'

The line straightened but Adam struck too late. The sun was coming out. For the first time, he saw a spark in Laura's eyes, as in the picture. Then a cloud covered the sun.

'It's cold, isn't it? Could you please kindly row me back to the boathouse.'

'Of course.' He reeled in the line and attached the fly to the rod.

As they approached the shore, Laura jumped out and waded in her town shoes and stockings. She stood on the bank as if about to say something.

'Laura, you don't need to say it.'

She seemed to want to speak and Adam thought he saw the spark come back into her eyes. But it was only the sun returning to the water. She began to run through the heather and then kneeled down and took off her wet shoes. Adam watched her till she was just a shiny red speck on the horizon.

CHAPTER FIFTEEN

It was the summer, the summer of all those big weddings, because Adam was abroad again, although where he was this time, of this nobody was quite sure. Not Lebanon, surely; David rather thought Algeria and Mary was too busy with the house to answer. Sir Donald knew, but Laura was distracted, and he did not mention Adam's name.

It was that summer of 198-, the summer after the war, for Adam was not simply abroad but sitting on the stone base of some palings outside the Central Post Office and holding an unopened letter. It was late afternoon and, at the school across the waste ground before him, loudspeakers were calling on the girls to veil while their chauffeurs chattered with the blind porter at the gate. Adam looked at the letter but hesitated before opening it. Lydia wrote regularly and once, even, Mrs Mark, telling him that Mary had been a little overwrought but was now fit as anything; but this was in a strange hand and twice re-addressed.

Adam was editor of the English-language newspaper. George had found him the job; or perhaps it was not his father but Butterworth, for both had claimed credit. Adam enjoyed the work. At first, the heat of the coast had oppressed him and he had not been able to sleep; but he was now used to it. He spent all day at the newspaper and sometimes was still there, at three o'clock in the morning, typing at the hot metal a late alteration to the splash. Then he would sigh, and breathing in the damp of early morning – it was never chill – he would throw a twist of paper at the Yemenite printer asleep on a sheet of newsprint. They were not allowed their weapons in this country but Adam never woke them suddenly.

It was a country of fabulous riches, but whether it was

Paradise, as its few citizens claimed, or Hell, as the Embassy ladies complained, Adam did not know. New cars were abandoned to gather white dust when their tanks were empty. Roads and bridges sprang up but led nowhere. Just before dawn, as he was driven home, Adam would sometimes find himself in suburbs he had not known existed. Returning at noon, he would come on cars smashed against lamp-posts, their occupants vanished and no blood on the road.

Music was not heard in public and the women went veiled, even these young girls now being shepherded to their chauffeurs by the blind porter. The men took early to corpulence and loathed to stir from their immense ramshackle houses unless to step into motor cars so garishly decorated as to seem mere extensions of the household.

Hell, surely; yet people came from every corner of the world and the port could not manage the traffic. The harbourmaster, who was a Lebanese since the local people did not like such work, confided that some shippers were sending unserviceable hulks to earn handsome demurrage at the end of the line of vessels. A prominent offender was Admiral Maritime Services Ltd, formerly of Beirut, now of the Minories, London.

The people seemed happy in their haggard land. Only in the hottest months would they leave the country, to behave execrably on the shores of the Mediterranean (although not, as before, in Lebanon). It was as if the stern laws of the land, which required execution for the slightest offence or lapse in manners, were abrogated at the breakwater. The prodigals returned in October, complaining bitterly of the high prices and indifferent service, as angels must after going among men.

Paradise, then; but not the paradise of the Christians with their last-minute scamper for salvation; not even the Jewish Promised Land which corrupts at attainment like a long-buried fresco exposed to air; nearer, if anything, to the peace of Islam, where there is no sin, only mistakes, no guilt but shame, and where a man may feel at home where he is.

Adam had no friends. Smith came with the Secretary of State, who was petitioning for a loan, but his programme was circumscribed and Adam dared not leave the Yemenites and visit the capital. They spoke on the telephone but not of the battle. The embassies invited Adam to parties for they wondered if his leaders might not express the views of the government in the Interior. Adam had visited the Minister of Religious Propagation, Shipping and National Economy on arrival, but after waiting three hours with his Egyptian secretary in the ante-room, they had tiptoed in to find the great man asleep behind a large pile of money. Adam wrote as he thought best.

One man he did visit. He was of the Embassy staff but lived some distance from the sandy compound of his colleagues. He had been recommended by Butterworth and had, among the books he had picked up for nothing in English cathedral towns, a remaindered copy of Adam's *The Historic Error*. Adam found these visits torture. He preferred to stay at home, playing Bellini's operas on an old mono gramophone. An Eritrean girl looked after the house and, sometimes, without warning, would stay the night and Adam would dream of cool horses under green trees.

One day, walking in the bazaar, Adam ran into the young man who had given him the hibiscus in Rouche. He tried to embrace him. Embarrassed, they fell to talking. He was an engineer. His card showed a company called Sud Engineering. Afterwards, whenever Adam saw someone he thought he knew, a slim young man in a large, green Chevrolet, a burly policeman bullying motorists or a fat man in a *Newsweek* tee-shirt seated outside an open grocery, he would limp across the road and hurry on.

Adam opened the letter:

The Old Golf Club
Weybridge
Surrey

Sunday, June 11

Dear Adam

How are you? You never write but I thought, all the same, you might like to hear about all that has happened.

Poppy sends her love. I am staying with her at the moment.

David and Mary got married at Helle. I thought it was a bit much because Poppy wasn't asked but Mary was very nice to me, asking me up to her room before they drove off and saying I was her best friend. I spent most of the time with Princess Margaret. The Marks gave them a Pontormo and the Lowestofts a fitted kitchen.

Laura behaved badly, as I knew she would, bursting into tears in the marquee and saying you had ruined Mary's life. She has been very odd since you left. On the anniversary of Toby's accident, Poppy and I gave a little party, just for his closest friends, to remember him with readings of poetry etc. Laura at first refused to come and then arrived in the middle and threw glasses around.

Perhaps it's not such a bad thing that she's going to live all the time in Scotland, though rather her than me, with that depressing old man. She refuses to believe that Johnny has gone off for good, just like her mother. Billy von Schlesien stopped at the island in his yacht and said they've gone crackers, going down every week to watch the boat from Oban come in.

The really exciting thing is that Poppy has agreed to be my wife! We decided at the Priory, where we went because she was rather tired and I was overworked at the office. We'll be getting married here next month. I don't expect you'll be able to get back so I won't send an invitation. Poppy has started a list at the General Trading Company in Sloane Street. I've invited Laura, so that bygones can be bygones, but she hasn't replied, which is typically rude. Don't tell anybody but you-know-who from Kensington Palace is coming.

We live much more quietly now, Poppy and I, and I wouldn't be surprised if we start a family quite quickly. I haven't seen Mary since she came back from Jerusalem with David although everybody says she's got very fat. She's so quiet that people say she's no fun any more. I'm sure they'll ask us down when they've got Bilston in order. She's supposed to have started her own gallery to deal in pictures with all David's money. Between you and me, she knows less about paintings than I do though the papers, of course, had to make a big thing about her finding the Reynolds of the fat woman with the child. She never denies to anyone about you-know-what which I think is stupid.

What a long letter! I'm working for Poppy's father in his shipbroking office at the moment but we'll be going into partnership as soon as possible, he says. I might even come and visit you in the desert!

Wish me good luck,

Cheers

Oliver

Adam stood up. The school was silent and barred. He set off down towards the harbour and, as he turned onto the Corniche with the sea on his right hand and the churning Lunapark in front of him, he assembled a parish of rich women. Adam walked on, past families picnicking under the palms and students reading under bent lamp-posts, and thought of Mary, Laura and Kate; and he went on walking and thinking of Mary, Kate and Laura, till night came down and the lights went up on the ships strung out for miles in the roads.